BLACK BUTTERFLY

Also by Mark Gatiss

The Vesuvius Club

The Devil in Amber

BLACK BUTTERFLY

A SECRET SERVICE THRILLER

MARK GATISS

SIMON &
SCHUSTER

London · New York · Sydney · Toronto

A CBS COMPANY

First published in Great Britain by Simon & Schuster UK Ltd, 2008
A CBS COMPANY

1 3 5 7 9 10 8 6 4 2

Simon & Schuster UK Ltd
1st Floor
222 Gray's Inn Road
London WC1X 8HB

www.simonsays.co.uk

Simon & Schuster Australia
Sydney

A CIP catalogue record for this book is available from the British Library

HB ISBN: 978-0-7432-5711-4
TPB ISBN: 978-0-7432-5712-1

Typeset in Times by M Rules
Printed in the UK by CPI Mackays, Chatham ME5 8TD

For Maurice – because dads, like diamonds, are forever

ACKNOWLEDGEMENTS

Grateful thanks to Caroline Chignell, Francesca Main, Joe Pickering, Julian Rhind-Tutt, Nigel Stoneman, Ben Willsher and especially Ian, as ever, with all my love.

CONTENTS

The Hammerhead's mouth was jagged as a knife-wound.

The ghostly form of the shark pressed itself against the wall of the glass tank, oblivious to the thrum of the generators and the pellucid light that dappled its pale flesh. Shadows moved like living things, leaping and sloping over the oppressively low ceiling and concrete walls of the Aquarium.

Lucifer Box was dead tired. He thrust two more Benzedrine tablets into his mouth, stepped closer to the creature's enclosure and watched his reflection balloon as though glimpsed in a fairground mirror. A step back and the reality snapped into focus: a tall, slim, saturnine figure in the clinging form of the Siebe Gorman wet-suit, the damp black hair scraped off the forehead, the cruel blue eyes dilated by the queasy gloom.

Stealthy as a cat, Box moved on, leaving wet footprints on the concrete. The heat was suffocating and beads of sweat stood out on his forehead like dew on a rose. He wiped them away with the back of one hand and swallowed, his mouth suddenly dry.

Damn her! Damn the blasted girl!

If it hadn't been for Stiletto he'd be out of Hong Kong now, settling down on the Cathay Pacific out of Kai Tak: catching the eye of a tulip-slim stewardess as he downed his third single malt. Looking forward to dear old rain-swept England and getting away, far away, from the sweaty horror that had been the search for Gottfried Clawhammer.

What a punishing three months it had been! From the freezing saltmines of Petrograd to the nightclubs of Macao and finally to a confrontation with Clawhammer himself: twenty stones of pallid flesh, the shaved head like a bullet, the eyes obscenely liquid just like those of the deep-sea creatures that twisted and writhed in this very Aquarium.

And then there was Stiletto, Clawhammer's mistress. Box recalled the moment he'd first seen her: blindingly beautiful, clad only in an ivory-coloured bathing costume, lying prone on the deck of the *Beguine*. As the yacht bobbed at anchor his eyes had devoured her. The long, lissom legs, the proud mound of the bikini, the perfect breasts in their pearly cups . . .

There was a movement to his right. Box tensed and took a swift step into the shadows, his hand closing on the comforting chill of the Beretta strapped to his waist. His eyes, mere slits beneath dark brows, narrowed further.

The sound had come from another tank, this one blooming with the pulsing plumpness of a dozen blue-ringed octopus. One, its suckers big as two-shilling pieces, was clamped to the glass. The creature seemed to consider Box with detachment, then, tentacles spreading like petals, it darted away into the cloudy water.

He moved silently on, the thrumming metronome of the generators keeping time with his own thumping heart. Shaking his head, he tried to clear the image of Stiletto from his mind. He needed to be alert now as never before. But the girl's shimmering beauty, the memory of her body – warm and urgent beneath his – jutted to the forefront of his mind like the Hammerhead against the glass wall of its prison.

Damn the silly bitch! She'd get such a spanking when all this was over.

Box shook his head and bit his lip. First they had to get out of there alive. And his plan? He had none.

Box's left hand, slippery with perspiration, clutched the solid plastic handle of the Leibach translator machine. The instrument was compact – about the size of a portable typewriter – and it was heavy. But it was the price of Stiletto's freedom.

He turned a corner and what he saw made his heart stop.

Yet another huge glass tank stood before him. Within, submerged and bound hand and foot, stood Stiletto. Big lead weights were roped about her waist, her feet firmly anchored to the white sand that lined the bottom of the tank. Where the ropes had chafed too tightly against her wrists, droplets of rusty blood rose lazily towards the surface like a rosary.

The girl's turquoise eyes bulged with fright behind a diving mask, the ugly rubber mouthpiece of an aqualung clamped between the perfect 'O' of her lips. She saw Box and tried to move, sending a stream of air bubbles rocketing to the surface.

'She is unharmed,' whispered a sibilant voice. 'Whether or not she remains so, Mr Box, is entirely dependent on you.'

Box whirled round but he could make out nothing in the stygian shadows.

The voice came again: 'Please put down your weapon.'

Box unholstered the Beretta and let it drop to the concrete.

'Kick it over to me.'

'I can't see where you are, damn it,' spat Box.

The softest of treads and suddenly the bloated shape of Gottfried Clawhammer glided from the gloom – like a conga eel from behind a nigger-head.

A ghastly smile, the blubbery lips peeling back to reveal tiny teeth. 'Now you see me.' Suddenly, from the sleeve of his well-cut kimono, the muzzle of an automatic protruded. 'Your gun, if you please.'

Box put one bare foot onto the Beretta and kicked it across to him. Clawhammer stooped to pick it up, opened the chamber and let the ammunition clatter to the floor. He tossed the useless weapon aside and, cocking his head to one side, looked Box up and down.

'I have enjoyed this game, Mr Box, and, though it grieves me to say it, you have beaten me. My little scheme to replace all the world's Swan Vestas with tiny sticks of nerve gas has, alas, failed.'

'You met your match,' said Box, with a small smile. 'Your pals in "Redland" aren't going to be very pleased, Clawham—'

'But there is still one ace up my sleeve,' cut in the whispering menace. His large round eyes swivelled in the direction of the tank. 'Miss Stiletto. Her body was pleasing to me in its way . . .'

Box's fists clenched.

'. . . but now she has a use beyond the merely physical. I calculate she has two more minutes of air, Mr Box. If you are quick, you may be able to prevent her from drowning. And whilst you are occupied, myself and the Leibach – such an ingenious device, don't you think? – will be racing towards the Chinese border. The Riva speedboat is outside, as instructed?'

Box gave a grudging nod.

'Good.' Clawhammer held out his free hand and the sleeve of the kimono gaped like the sickle-mouth of the Hammerhead. 'The translator, if you please.'

Box stiffened with fury. There had to be a way out of this. *Had* to be!

He threw a frantic glance at the girl in the tank, whose eyes had taken on a desperate appeal. Her hands restrained and thus unable to gesture, Stiletto was urgently dipping her head towards the dials on the aqualung. The air was fast running out. Box nodded.

'If you're going to go, you bastard, then go,' he barked, sliding the Leibach along the floor, in the same direction he had sent his pistol.

The big man carefully crouched down and grunted as he picked up the device. 'I've never cared for goodbyes,' he sighed, lips smacking wetly over his grey teeth. 'But I do have a little parting gift for you.'

His hand moved swiftly, and wrenched a nearby lever. Something whooshed down a concealed chute, hitting the water like a bullet, and there was a sudden flurry of movement in the tank. A flash in the water, bright as silver, then a wall of glittering shapes soon resolved into the ugly gun-metal grey of a shoal of fish.

Piranha!

Stiletto's eyes widened in stark terror.

Box froze. He was dimly aware of a soft, clapping tattoo that he realised must be the sound of Clawhammer's sandals on the concrete as the thug made his escape. But Box made no move to follow. All that mattered now was the girl.

The piranha swirled about Stiletto as though in a vortex. Disorientated for now by their journey down the chute and into the tank, they would soon begin to explore their new environment. To nudge and nip at Stiletto's soft flesh and then –

Oh God. The blood!

The girl was already bleeding from the ropes at her wrists. Once the deadly fish tasted that . . .

Box knew he had very little time. His eyes searched desperately for some kind of weapon to shatter the tank. If he could manage that, then all their problems would be solved at one stroke: the piranha rendered impotent, the girl able to breathe fresh air. But there was nothing heavy to be seen, nothing but the endless glass rectangles of the Aquarium. If only he still had the Beretta . . .

In the tank, Stiletto squirmed. The more she panicked, the quicker she would use up her precious air. She struggled at the thick ropes that bound her, hair streaming upwards like golden seaweed.

If only he still had the Beretta . . .

And then realisation came like a punch on the jaw. Clawhammer had emptied the pistol but had discarded it on the Aquarium floor. Even as Box darted into the shadows in search of the gun, he saw, with a throb of nausea, the first piranha taking an exploratory nibble at the girl's wrist.

Dropping to his knees, he fanned out his hands, groping in the darkness. Nothing. Nothing but the cracked concrete, sticky with stagnant water and gently humming with the noise of the generators. Then his racing heart seemed to stop as he suddenly grasped the reassuring bulk of the Beretta's butt, its chamber still open, whirring round as his hand clutched the weapon.

He cracked shut the chamber, leaped to his feet, dashed to the tank and slammed the pistol against the glass.

A dull *thunk*. He tried again, harder, harder. Then with desperation, smashing the weapon harmlessly against the unyielding surface.

Box clenched his teeth in frustration. He was a fool! The glass would be toughened to withstand the incredible pressure of the water. This wasn't like breaking through a blasted pantry window!

The sight of Stiletto's lithe form amidst the swirling horror of the piranha shoal made him redouble his efforts, belting at the impervious tank, hoping against hope for penetration.

And now two or three of the hideous creatures were clustering around Stiletto's arm, gnawing at the white flesh. The stream of blood steadily grew. Box felt his stomach flip.

Stiff with fear, air bubbles frothing from her mouthpiece, Stiletto thrashed her lovely head from side to side. '*No hope*,' she seemed to be saying. '*No hope, no hope . . .*'

But Box was already on the flat of his Neoprene-clad

stomach, hands turned into scrabbling claws as he sought out the missing bullets. Even as he searched, his gaze kept flicking upwards at the tank. At the oxygen dial and the needle that hovered over zero. At the hideous dazzle of the lethal fish, deadly teeth working even as their cold, doll's eyes flashed in the half-light . . .

And then – *thank Christ!* – his fingers found a bullet, chill on the concrete.

In one practised move, Box flicked open the chamber of the Beretta, thrust the bullet home, shut the chamber, jumped up, aimed and fired.

The plate glass shattered with a massive percussion. At once, water vomited through the gaping hole, sending the piranha flapping and gasping into the foetid air.

Stiletto collapsed at once, and Box rocketed forward, using the gun to smash at the remaining glass. He climbed into the tank. Holding on to her tightly, he ripped the rubber mask from her deathly pale face. The remaining water sloshed about their ankles.

Box ignored the bloodied ropes and the leaden weights that held the girl down. He cradled her face in his hands and smoothed the soaking blonde hair from her eyes. Her lips were blue, her skin snow-cold.

'Come on!' he yelled at her. 'Come on! Breathe! Breathe!'

He shook her like a limp doll. Then, suddenly, she gasped and retched, doubling up in his arms. Her eyes rolled down. Bloodshot and brimming with tears, but still beautiful to behold.

For a moment, she looked unseeingly at him. Then she

smiled. 'Oh, Lucifer. I knew you would come. I knew you would save me.'

Box found his hand straying to the insistent curve of her breast – then, cursing himself, he pulled away. But Stiletto had other ideas. She feebly took hold of his hand and returned it to her chest. Box felt the nipple rise and harden.

'No,' he said shortly. 'You need to rest. And I have to get after Clawhammer and that damned Leibach.'

She shook her head, strands of damp hair clinging to her porcelain features. 'Later. *Later.* Please. For now there is only us. I want you to love me, Lucifer Box. I want you to spank me. Love me and spank me. To make love to me as if I was a beast. The lowest beast in—'

.1.
BELIEVED EXTINCT

'BOX? *Box, old man! Shake a leg!*'

I opened my eyes wide and blinked once. Twice.

Bewildered, I glanced about. Olive-green walls, a hissing gas fire. A cabbagey smell like a school dormitory. There was a loud creak as I straightened in the chair, though whether it was the cracked leather or my hips, I'm not sure.

It took a moment to orientate myself. Through the dirty window, the sky was a grey smudge. Bowler-hatted commuters surged past an austere arched entrance, an occasional red bus breaking the monochrome tide, like a speck of blood in a black eye.

London.

No sharks. No piranha. No pneumatic girls in shattered Hong Kong fish-tanks. Nor any of that stuff hammered out on Remingtons by ex-foreign correspondents in seersucker shirts.

I scowled at the portrait of the new Queen gazing down from the wall, as though blaming her for puncturing my dreaming. My *lurid* dreaming, I have to say. There's no other word for it.

'What?' I said at last.

'The sainted Miss Beveridge is asking whether you'd like a cup of rosie,' said Allan Playfair, his voice as high and bright as ice plinking into a glass. He had one thumb on a grey intercom button.

I shook my head. 'Any coffee?'

Playfair pulled a face. 'Oh, Lord. Now you're asking. Got some Camp – any good?' I shook my head again. 'As for the real thing,' he chuckled, clamping his jaw onto the stem of a blackened pipe, 'easier to find Christine Jorgensen's nethers, old love.'

Playfair was about forty-five, with a utilitarian face and a suit as badly cut as his salt and pepper hair. He shifted uncomfortably within Prince of Wales check as he leaned towards the intercom and grunted: 'No tea.'

'Righto,' came Miss Beveridge's throaty Northern vowels from the outer office. Almost immediately, the machine sparked into life again, giving a rasp like a miner's lung. Playfair's face crumpled, irritated. 'Hold my calls,' he barked. Then he sat back and beamed at me.

'You shouldn't have let me drop off like that,' I said. 'Damned embarrassing – snoozing in someone else's office.'

'Seemed a shame to wake you,' he grinned. 'You looked so peaceful. And who wouldn't get a little drowsy after a slap-up nosh like that?'

I recalled with a shudder the wet lettuce and scalpel-thin ham that had passed for lunch.

'Besides . . .' Playfair went on, flipping open a pewter cigarette case and offering me a spindly fag. Strands of tobacco tumbled out.

'Besides?'

He relit his pipe and then extinguished the match in a couple of swift swoops. 'Well, you've earned a rest.'

'Oh, don't say that, for God's sake. Makes me sound . . .' I sighed and Playfair's brows rose. 'I could always take being envied,' I continued, 'or feared. But the one thing I never thought I'd be was *venerable*.'

He laughed explosively, his pipe jutting upwards so that the bowl almost touched his nose. 'That,' he coughed, 'you will never be. Monks are venerable, old love. Oxbridge dons, too. But a scoundrel like you? I think not.'

He chuckled again – rather hatefully. I said nothing.

Allan Playfair was a dependable chap. Solid. Respectable. And about to replace me.

Me.

The man who'd prevented the revivified zombie of Captain Scott destroying New Zealand with his steam-dreadnought the *Terror Nova*. The man who'd pursued and destroyed Dr Cassivelaunus Fetch and A.C.R.O.N.I.M. – the Anarcho-Criminal Retinue of Nihilists, Incendiarists and Murderers. The man who'd come out of the Second World War covered in glory (and certain unmentionables) after preventing the Nazis from exploding a miniature purgative inside the Prime Minister's guts.

I had risen to the top of my curious profession (oh, for goodness sake, I'm not going into all that again. Visit the library!). I was officially 'Joshua Reynolds', President of the Royal Academy. Not the oh-so-respectable bastion of Fine Art you might be imagining, of course, but the front for Her Britannic Majesty's really, *really* Secret Service. (There, I've said it. No need to go to the library now. I've saved you the bus fare.)

But to my old friends, old lovers, old tailors but most especially, dear old Reader, to you, I remain Lucifer Box.

Would you know me, still? The tall frame a little stooped in the black linen suit, the hands knotty with veins. Perhaps the eyes would still surprise you. Sharp and brightly blue, like the sun-glistened edge of a melting snowdrift. Or do I flatter myself? *Probably*.

My scandalous career had been quite a ride but, like all good things, had to come to an end. The Royal Academy was finally to be absorbed by the traditional MI6 mob: the 'Service'. With their checkpoints and their microfilmed sex-acts and their shabby little assassinations in rainy Czech alleys.

Playfair held up a hand. 'Anyway, I'm in no rush, old love. You remember that. You have all the time in the world.'

'One month,' I said, contemplating the popping gas-fire. It was a stiflingly hot June, but Playfair was notoriously thin-blooded. 'It really doesn't take that long to clear one's desk.'

'What have you got on, anyway?' he asked. 'Something juicy, I trust? Something nice for me to inherit? Or are you going to sort everything out in four short weeks and leave me with slim pickings?'

'I'm winding down gently . . .' I began.

'Out with it!'

'Well . . .'

'I knew it, you old fox!'

I shrugged. 'Something down in Cape Town. Locals have been looking for Coelacanth.'

'Beg pardon?'

'Species of ancient fish,' I explained. 'Long believed extinct but still hanging around.'

We both smiled at that.

'Well,' I continued, 'the Cape Towners caught something all right, but it wasn't what it appeared.'

Playfair rubbed his hands together. 'Don't tell me! A robotic Soviet listening device covered in scales and fins!'

'Nothing so interesting. Just a body. An old friend of mine, in point of fact.'

He stopped sucking on his pipe. 'Oh, I am sorry. What happened?'

I shrugged. 'Looks like suicide. Drove his car into the bay.'

Playfair shook his head. 'Bloody shame.' He got up and started opening drawers. 'Tell you what. I think there might still be some sherry here somewhere. Left over from the Coronation.'

'No, thanks. And how about you?'

'Hm?'

'Cases? Pending?'

Playfair pulled a face. 'Usual pallid guff. Chinese making ugly noises. Narcotics scare out in the Balkans'. He paused with a dusty bottle of Sandeman in one hand. 'Leftist grumblings in Venezuela . . .'

I nodded dully.

The parp of car horns and the unmistakable roar of the city sent a sudden and unexpected pang of emotion surging through me. I glanced round at the drearily respectable portraits and the drearily respectable room. 'I just hope . . .'

'Yes?'

'I just hope you have some *fun*,' I said. 'It really used to be the most tremendous fun.'

'Don't think I signed the chit for "fun",' said Playfair. He smiled and raised his glass. 'To you.'

He got to his feet and buttoned his jacket. 'Well, if you'll excuse me. Pleasure, as always. And I'm sure I'll see you again before you leave.'

'If you like.'

'Cheerio, old love.' He took my hand and then glanced down at the desk, his attention already elsewhere. For all his bonhomie, I had been effectively dismissed.

I went through into the outer office, a smaller, darker, cooler version of Playfair's. Miss Beveridge looked up from her desk and smiled.

Ah, Miss Beveridge.

Charming girl. Carrying out her sherpa-like duties for the Service without a word of complaint. Padding up and down the olive-green corridors with buff files under both arms. Scribbling memos, delivering dockets. For a short while, she'd been seconded to the Royal Academy and that's when yours truly, never content to doze off into a copy of *Art and Artists* when there's something delicious about, had noticed other things about Miss Beveridge. I'd observed her long, lovely neck, for instance, startlingly brown against the crisp white of her lace collar; the way her eyes disappeared into crinkled half-moons when she smiled; her infectious and frankly dirty Lancastrian chuckle. In addition, having studied dusty files of my adventures in her youth, she was a dedicated fan. Perhaps, over a Madeira or four, I could immerse myself in a very different Beveridge Report . . .

'The young lad's here, sir,' she said brightly.

I had lost myself in dreaming again. 'Is he? Right. Thank you, Beveridge.'

'Smashing to see you again, Mr Box.'

'And you, my dear.'

As she began shuffling papers, I gazed at her. Slender, exquisitely coiffured and perfect. I was fooling myself. What the deuce would someone like her see in old Lucifer Box? An indulgent smile was all I would ever get.

But as I moved to the door, she looked up again.

'Sir? I just wanted to say good luck, sir. And . . . well, it won't be the same without you.'

'Thanks.' I felt suddenly emboldened. Perhaps the party wasn't over just yet. 'Um . . . I was wondering . . . I have an appointment tomorrow. Rather a depressing matter, I'm afraid. Funeral. Old friend.'

'Oh, I'm sorry to hear that, sir.'

'Well, I was wondering whether you'd be available to accompany me? Hate to go to these things alone. Then, perhaps, a spot of lunch? And I can regale you with tales of some of my more sensational past glories.'

To my delight, the girl's face lit up. 'Oh, that'd be grand, Mr Box!'

'Splendid.'

'I can drive us there, if you like,' she enthused. 'I've nowt flash, mind, in the car department.'

'That's perfectly all right. It's Number Nine, Downing Street.'

'Yes, I know that bit,' she chuckled.

'Shall we say eleven o'clock?'

Miss Beveridge nodded enthusiastically and, with as much insouciance as I could muster, I left the office and made my way down the peeling stairwell, grinning like a youngster and positively dancing on air.

Awaiting me at the entrance was a little boy. He was sitting on a bench, legs sticking out before him like two white poles in neat grey socks. A beret covered most of the thick blue-black coils of his hair. He looked up as I approached but didn't smile.

'Good afternoon, Christmas,' I sighed.

'Hello, Daddy,' he said.

.2.
SCOUTING FOR BOYS

The Scouting Association has never held much appeal for me. I've no truck with paramilitary organisations. Way back in the mists, mind you, when the old Queen was happy and fairly glorious, I did have some slight acquaintance with Baden-Powell. Though quite why the defender of Mafeking devoted his declining years to all those athletic young lads – *well* – you have to wonder.

However, my son Christmas had taken to Scouting with almost indecent fervour, and was forever knotting Sheepshanks, sparking up campfires and shinning up those ropes with waxy ends you find dangling in chilly school gymnasia. He'd done so well, indeed, that he was to participate in some sort of International Camp and it was my duty, on that sultry afternoon, to set him on his way.

I didn't have the heart to tell him some of the things I'd done for International Camp but then fathers and sons shouldn't have those sorts of conversations, should they?

I'm getting ahead of myself, though.

Christmas Box – you didn't see that one coming, did you? The product of too much Montrachet and a broken axle on the road to Zagreb, he was an indiscretion that didn't even have the excuse of being youthful. One really doesn't expect bundles to turn up on one's doorstep on frosty Yuletide Eves, when the heat is in the very sod and one is entertaining a plumber's mate in the pantry (I bat for both the First and Second Eleven, if you recall). But that's exactly what had happened. Several urgent tugs – at the doorbell, you understand – summoned me to the front door and I'd grumpily left off the plumb-bob. In the snow outside I found a tiny child with a gently snubbed nose and the brightest boot-button eyes. Tied to his toe was a scribbled shipping label in the clumsy hand of the Zagrebian temptress, explaining all.

I'd done the decent thing – for once in my life – and given the brat my name, plus another in honour of the season (I was never going to call him Noel, was I?), then packed him off to some ancient boarding school for his betterment. On high days and holidays, I was obliged to take him out for an airing.

Despite my best efforts at succouring his artistic soul, Christmas had sat glumly through various exhibitions and museum trips, only brightening at the prospect of a knee-grazing trip to the park. I fear that, like his mother, he had an unhealthy interest in outdoor pursuits.

The little squib was forever complaining that everything was awfully boring and why couldn't we go and see some racing cars down at Brooklands or something? Finally, in a kind of desperate parental funk, I had enrolled the lad in the Scouts.

Well, that's not strictly accurate. For, with National Service winding down and Teddy Boys slashing up the upholstery in crumbling picture-houses, the dib-dib-dibbers had been reborn as the grandly titled 'New Scout Movement'. The great unwashed had seized on this with fervour, gleefully stuffing thousands of their grisly offspring into camps where they could expend all their pent-up energy washing Morris Travellers and helping veterans of El Alamein across the road. Its Honorary Chairman was the much-loved Lord Battenburg and it was a real force for good, according to the *Daily Mail* – although that's rarely a happy sign.

To me it all sounded horribly healthy and well-intentioned but then, as you may know, I had a depraved childhood.

For some unfathomable reason, the whole summer knees-up was set to kick off on one of those queer little islands that squat in the outer reaches of the Thames. Christmas and I motored through Town and then headed south through Richmond until we came to a crumbling wooden footbridge that connected the mainland to the island.

The bruised sky threatened thunder.

Christmas, looking like a little lead soldier in his navy-blue coat, stomped boldly over the bridge and past scrubby outcrops of leafless bushes. We then crossed a second, more substantial bridge, over a weir, where water thundered down in plumes.

'Come *on*, Daddy,' mewled Christmas. 'We'll be late. Miss ffawthawte says that punctuality is a virtue.'

'Oh, does she now?' I grumbled. I was already conjuring visions of flyblown church halls and pallid youths in vests doing physical jerks. Which is not nearly as much fun as jerking physical youths in vests, pallid or otherwise. 'I'm sure whatever wonders they have in store, they'll keep. And who is this Miss . . . what did you say she was called?'

'Miss ffawthawte,' piped the boy. 'You *know*. She's the one who got me started.'

'I thought *I* was the one who got you started.'

'You just signed the forms.'

'So I did.' With a heavy heart and not in the least interested, I pushed open a sagging wooden gate marked *Private*.

Beyond lay a broad meadow, dotted with pyramid-shaped tents and small wooden houses, jetties leading from each to the river. The pathway was overhung by weeping willows. From beneath one of them, a woman in a well-cut skirt and jacket suddenly appeared.

I took in her steel spectacles and a heart-shaped face of alabaster loveliness. Lustrous burnt-sienna curls hung to her shoulders. Only a tiny scar just above the mouth marred the perfection. A hare-lip, clearly, though long ago put right. By her parents, I wondered – or by an altruistic lover?

The newcomer extended a slim white hand.

'Melissa ffawthawte,' she purred. 'You must be Mr Box. I'm *very* pleased to meet you.'

'My absolute pleasure,' I said silkily, straightening up and smoothing down my waistcoat.

'And here's my little Christmas!' She planted a hand on the top of the boy's beret and he beamed up at her. 'We are all thrilled and honoured to have such a clever young man as part of our team.' Her green eyes widened. 'You must be very proud.'

'Oh, bursting with it,' I lied. 'Positively bursting.'

Miss ffawthawte pushed an errant curl from her face. I couldn't keep my eyes off the tiny pulse beating in her pale throat. She had the look of a girl I'd fox-trotted across the floor at Maxim's on Armistice Day, 1918. What a night! The Germans hadn't been the only ones to surrender.

'To get this far, Mr Box,' said Miss ffawthawte, 'your son has passed a huge number of tests and obstacles.'

'Has he?' I said, pulling a face. 'Dear me. Sounds rather like schoolwork! Are you sure you didn't mind, Christmas?'

The boy shrugged and gazed up at Melissa ffawthawte with cow-eyes. 'I didn't mind.'

She took off his beret and stroked his head. 'Now, at last, he has joined the elite. The cream.'

'How lovely for him,' I said. 'I shall rely on you to ensure that he doesn't curdle.'

The beauty managed a small smile and I felt encouraged, just as I had been by Miss Beveridge's response. This was more like it! If not exactly *raging* against the dying of the light, I was at least a little cross with it. Miss ffawthawte ushered us on down the path.

All around the meadow, bell-shaped tents had been erected and there was that pervasive grassy smell one associates with village fêtes and flower shows. Each tent swarmed with athletic-looking youngsters in khaki shorts and absurd sombrero-like hats. I was suddenly rather uncomfortably reminded of another youth group which had gained some little popularity in thirties Nuremberg.

'You must forgive my ignorance,' I said, stepping carefully

over a guy-rope, 'but this camp of yours – what exactly goes on?'

'You were never a Scout, Mr Box?' enquired Miss ffawthawte.

I chuckled. 'No, I—'

'After your time, of course,' she cut in. 'What a shame.' Tilting her head, she appraised me with the sort of pitying look that is the special preserve of youth. Miss ffawthawte and her Teutonic tonic, I thought, could stand a little puncturing.

'You have funny names, don't you,' I said cheerily, 'for the wallahs in charge of it all? Something from Kipling, isn't it – the Kim, the Baloo?'

'Akela.'

'The Mowgli?'

'*Akela*,' she repeated, with depressing earnestness, rouged mouth setting into a firm line.

'That's the chap.' I looked around. 'Is he about?'

Miss ffawthawte shook her head. 'Not at present. We're very busy – as you can imagine.'

'Oh, I'm sure,' I chuckled. 'All that pop to uncork. But you understand I must be content that my boy is in safe hands.'

'Don't you worry about a thing, Mr Box,' she said, fondling Christmas's hair. 'We'll take the best care of him. The very *best.* I wasn't fortunate enough to have such opportunities when I was a girl, so now I'm keen to spread some of my good fortune around.'

'Very laudable. I'm sure he'll have marvellous fun.'

'Fun, yes,' said Miss ffawthawte, gazing down into the lad's eyes. 'But he'll also learn lots of new and exciting things. Our charges must "be prepared" in all things. That's what we're all about.' She looked into the middle distance. 'It will be a great Movement.'

'I always say it's important to manage a great Movement at least once a day.'

Her green eyes narrowed. 'Great because young people,' she said silkily, 'are the future, are they not?'

'Well, there's no arguing with that,' I said. 'They'll still be here, long after we're dust.'

Miss ffawthawte gave me a look over her steel spectacles that seemed to say: 'Long after *some* of us are dust.'

'So,' I said, moving on in the hope of speeding up the whole wretched parental business. 'When does everyone arrive for the knees-up?'

Miss ffawthawte crossed her hands in front of her. 'The Jamboree begins next week. In Kingston.'

'Super,' I said distractedly, imagining how disappointed all those foreign Scouts would be with suburban little Kingston-on-Thames. But no doubt gallons of ginger beer and pickled eggs would put them right.

We were approaching a large dark hut, constructed from logs in that quaint fashion one associates with spa towns and skiing resorts. It was exactly the sort of lifeless place I had expected and, once we were through the double doors, I took in the noticeboards covered with neatly typed announcements, the stacks of tubular chairs and a slightly crippled ping-pong table under a tin lampshade. The place stank of damp.

A long corridor stretched off immediately in front of us, the windows inset in it looking into cheaply panelled rooms. From the blur of white vests and navy-blue pants within, it seemed the Scouts were engaged in vigorous exercise.

I was about to look away when I became aware that someone was watching us through one of the interior windows. I took a step back.

It was a strange and sickly boy, hollow-eyed and jaundiced-looking, like the ghost of a Victorian child drowned in a weir. Limp yellow hair slimed its way across the pale forehead, and his arms and legs were pathetically shrivelled in indigo pants and a startlingly white vest.

He stared at me unblinkingly and I had the oddest feeling I'd seen him somewhere before. Then he was gone, swallowed up in the mass of spotty youth tearing excitedly round the room.

'Can I go now?' piped up Christmas.

I glanced down and his face was shining with excitement. Well, if the little scrap wanted to volunteer for all this leaping about and frog-spawn collecting, who was I to gainsay him? I bent down and was all too aware of the pistol-shot cracking of my joints.

'Have a lovely time, Christmas,' I murmured, awkwardly patting my child on the head. 'Don't get into any trouble now, promise?'

His bright gaze was straying already to the back of the hut. He looked at me crossly. 'Of course I won't.'

My temper flared, but Miss ffawthawte intervened, dragging the boy behind her back. 'I'll just settle him in, Mr Box,' she said quickly. 'And then perhaps I can show you the rest of the camp.'

I nodded. 'Yes, please. I can't wait to see your . . . facilities.'

She met my gaze. 'Oh, they don't disappoint, I can assure you. I won't be a moment. I'll meet you down the corridor. Third room on the left. Say goodbye to your father, Christmas.'

The boy peeped round her skirts and mouthed, 'Bye.'

I waved at the boy, feeling a sudden, disturbing pang of what I dimly recognised as guilt.

Miss ffawthawte took his hand and turned to go.

'Oh, by the way,' I said. 'Third room on the left. What's in there?'

'The Games Room, Mr Box,' she said coolly. 'Do you like to play games?'

.3.
KISSING THE PINK

In stark contrast to the rest of the gimcrack establishment, the Games Room, which smelled pleasingly of beeswax, was in exceptional order. Tennis racquets in wooden frames lined the panelled walls, and well-polished shields commemorated past glories on the field. A pile of laced leather footballs, brown and shiny as conkers, had been built into a tidy pyramid below.

In pride of place, above the shields, was a photograph of the Movement's Honorary Chairman, Lord Battenburg. The tanned, smiling face of the famous scientist and adventurer gazed down serenely, as though offering benediction on the sporting enterprise to which the place was dedicated.

Dominating the room, however, was a splendid snooker table, the baize glowing a grassy green under the lampshades. In the centre, the glinting red balls lay neatly arranged in their wooden triangle, the colours on their spots, the white standing free. I crossed to the table, and set the lone white ball spinning. The gentle whirl it made on the cloth was curiously satisfying.

I removed a cue from the rack close by, and ran it experimentally between my thumb and forefinger.

The soft click of the door announced Melissa ffawthawte's entrance and in the dim light, she looked even more alluring. She removed her spectacles and her green eyes flashed. Within the masculine cut of her jacket, her breasts were shadowed into a deep V. Just visible was the frilled edge of a white brassière and, on the soft skin of her bosom, a curved black mark. I realised with a thrill that it was some kind of tattoo. I entertained the notion that, had Scout leaders been of Miss ffawthawte's stamp, I might have shown an interest much earlier.

'Very impressive,' I said, not entirely alluding to the Games Room.

'Akela provides in so many ways,' she enthused, closing the door behind her. 'He's a great believer in the power of play.'

'Oh, me too,' I said, then tapped the cue lightly on the table. 'This your game?'

'I'm sorry?'

'Snooker. It's an unlikely sport for a young lady, but in the absence of a draughts board . . .'

Miss ffawthawte ran her fingers over the reds, and they clicked and clacked as her nails stroked each one. 'I'm adept in most sports, Mr Box,' she said sweetly, 'but I must admit to a particular fondness for this one.' She lifted the triangle and the reds were exposed, like a segment of pomegranate seeds. 'And you? Are you *au fait* with it?'

I shrugged. 'Played a frame or two in my time.'

'Red ball, followed by all fifteen blacks until cleared. Then all the colours.'

I nodded. 'If one is lucky.'

'One makes one's own luck, don't you think?' Suddenly, she picked out a cue. 'Shall we toss?'

I refrained from the obvious rejoinder and, nodding, pulled a two-bob bit from my trousers. 'Call.'

'Tails.'

I flipped the florin. 'Tails it is. Just the one frame?'

The girl looked up. 'Oh, I think that's all I'll need.'

'Confident, aren't you, Miss ffawthawte?'

She didn't respond, but simply slipped off her jacket and hung it on a peg behind the door. The pointy brassière was visible now through the high-collared blouse.

'So,' I said. 'The stakes?'

Miss ffawthawte glanced at me and the faint scar above her lip caught the light of the shaded lamp. 'If you win,' she said matter-of-factly, 'the rewards would be great.'

'You don't say.'

'But you won't win, Mr Box.' Without hesitation, she positioned the white ball and, bending low with the cue, sent it cracking expertly into the crowd of reds. They broke beautifully. One immediately rolled to the bottom left pocket and sank without a sound. At once, Miss ffawthawte crouched down again, her rear turned rather pleasingly towards me, trim and firm beneath the short grey skirt. She sank the black without blinking.

'*Played*,' I muttered, tapping my cue against the floor. I adjusted the metal scorer on the wall and then went to replace the black on its spot. However, the girl was already on the move, eyes flickering back and forth as she scanned the table.

Then she was down again, the cue swished and another red was gone, then another black. I stayed by the scorer and she squeezed past me. I noticed the dark seams of her stockings.

The next shot wasn't quite so easy – the only pottable red was effectively hidden behind the green ball. I ran my hand up and down my cue, confident that I'd soon be at the table. Miss ffawthawte ducked down to retrieve one of the rests from beneath the baize, slotted her cue into the X at its tip and, with a sound like snapping teeth, swerved the white ball brilliantly around the green, sending the red whispering into the top right pocket.

I cleared my throat. She was good. She was *very* good.

'You see, Mr Box,' she murmured, never taking her eyes off the table, 'it's all a matter of angles. It's a beautiful game. A perfect game. If one can get the geometry right . . .' she stretched across the table and sent down another black '. . . there's no reason at all why one shouldn't win. Every time.'

I pulled absently at my ear-lobe, fascinated by this spirited female. 'Certainly, certainly. But it's not all science, Miss ffawthawte. I still say there's the matter of luck.'

She didn't answer, merely returned to the table and sent yet another red to its grave. I moved the score counter again. At this rate, I wasn't going to get any kind of a look-in. Another black, another red. The balls zoomed towards the pockets as though magnetically attracted. The points mounted inexorably.

'Speaking of angles' I said at last, as she whacked the black into the top right pocket. 'What's yours?'

She brushed a coil of hair from her eyes but didn't look up from her cueing. 'What do you mean?'

'You seem a very capable young woman to be mouldering away in a Scout camp,' I said quietly. 'What's in it for you?'

The cue shushed between her fingers. The white smacked into the red but it made an ugly noise.

The ball hit the cushion and bounced off.

I held my breath as the red sailed towards the bottom left pocket. Melissa ffawthawte didn't move, gripping her cue like a javelin. The ball rolled towards the open jaws of the pocket and she smiled. Then it glanced against the cushion, wobbled – and stopped dead.

The girl looked at it in abject disbelief.

'Oh, shame,' I said. 'Sounded like a mis-cue. *Here.*' I picked up the cube of blue chalk from the table and threw it over to her. 'You probably need this.'

She caught the cube, glared at it as though it were a burning coal, then hurled it back at me. The chalk bounced off my black linen, leaving a blue smear. I stooped to pick it up. 'Suit yourself.' After brushing it over the tip of my own cue, I stuffed the block into my trouser pocket and readied myself for my first shot of the match.

The girl stepped back from the table, glowering. Her gaze flickered over the view of the baize. Seventy-two points scored. A possible seventy-five points on the table. Could I claw my way back?

'Wish me luck,' I said happily, bending over the table and, with tremendous care, lining up the shot. I sent the white gently towards the nearest pottable red. There was a soft *clock* and it disappeared into the pocket. I moved swiftly round to work out the angle on the black. It shone like an olive under the lamplight.

This was a pretty easy shot, but those can be traps for the unwary so I took my time, sliding the cue back and forth, back and forth, between my thumb and finger, before neatly pocketing the ball. Melissa ffawthawte never took her eyes off me. I sent down another two reds, another two blacks.

I played steadily, unflashily. More reds sank. More blacks.

The girl remained silent, no sign of emotion other than the impatient rotation of the cue in her hand.

I knocked down a difficult red – and then an awkward ricochet got me into trouble.

I paused and hugged the cue to my chest, chewing my lip thoughtfully. I'd clawed my way to forty-one points against her seventy-two. I could still win.

The black ball was close to the top left-hand pocket, the blue not far away. However, the white had settled so close to the pink – I shaded my eyes and peered down at it to make sure – that it was what is called a *touching ball.* In other words, I would have to send the white rocketing away from the pink to avoid hitting it and making a foul, thus handing my opponent the upper hand and, very probably, the match.

Melissa ffawthawte leaned against the panelled walls, one finger placed idly on the metal scorer. 'Oh dear,' she murmured. 'And you were doing so well.'

To my surprise, I found my heart was racing and I took a few deep breaths to calm myself. After all, it was only a game. There was nothing at stake except my pride.

I drummed my fingers against the cushion. Somewhere a clock chimed.

There was just a chance that, if I could put enough screw on the white ball as I cued it away from the pink, it might curve round and sink the black into the pocket. I wiped perspiration from my forehead and looked again at the balls: the black on the jaws of the pocket, the pink and the white cheek-by-jowl close by.

I took the chalk from my pocket and stroked it distractedly once, twice, three times over the tip of the cue. Then I put the little cube back in my trousers and bent down to play the shot.

Holding the cue high, as though spearing a fish, I brought it down with tremendous power onto the top of the white. There was a curious noise, like marbles jostling together. Too hard! I'd hit the damn thing too hard!

The ball raced away down the table and hit the far cushion.

Melissa ffawthawte made a tiny, excited noise in her throat.

But the strength with which I'd hit the ball meant that it bounced off the cushion and veered back up the table.

It rolled – rolled – rolled – and hit the black!

My heart leaped.

The black collided with the blue but revolved towards the pocket.

I swallowed. My throat was like paper.

The ball rotated on its axis like a tiny planet, hovered in the soft green jaws – and stopped.

My face fell.

Melissa ffawthawte whooped with joy. She threw her cue into the air and caught it again – but I suddenly stayed her with a gesture and pointed to the table.

Because the disturbed blue ball was still travelling.

As we watched, it rolled softly, gently, towards the middle pocket and – with an understated *clunk* – vanished from sight.

I burst into spontaneous laughter. The blue ball was worth five points! I could still win! I didn't even look at Miss ffawthawte as I cleared the rest of the table swiftly and efficiently: yellow, green, brown, blue, pink and the final black, a tinglingly satisfying long pot that travelled smoothly down the baize into the bottom right pocket.

There was a deathly silence.

Then Melissa ffawthawte swung towards me, eyes blazing. She took her cue in both hands and, with a snarl of rage, snapped it in two. Whitish splinters peppered the green cloth of the table.

'Congratulations,' she managed.

I shrugged. 'Well, you know. Just a fluke.' I held out my hand. 'I enjoyed that. Perhaps we can play again some time.'

She looked down at my hand as though it was some species of crawling reptile, then moved towards the door.

'Oh,' I said. 'I believe there was some talk of a prize?'

Melissa ffawthawte turned in the doorway. 'Perhaps, Mr Box,' she hissed, 'you'll find your reward in heaven.'

She stalked from the room, slamming the door behind her.

Stepping outside, I made my way back through the camp, happy as Larry, buoyed by my narrow victory. I barely registered the industrious activity of the Scouts thronging the meadow. By the time I'd reached the footbridge, my mind was already focusing, with delicious anticipation, on the next day and my appointment with Miss Beveridge. Then, with a jolt, I reminded myself of the reason for our meeting. The interment of Christopher Miracle.

.4.
SNOBBERY WITH VIOLETS

'Funerals, it may surprise you to learn, my dear Miss Beveridge, are awfully sexy.'

'Sir?'

I checked my appearance in the hall mirror, carefully placing a sombre Homburg onto my white locks. The girl had arrived precisely on time the next morning, pulling up outside Number Nine, Downing Street in a black Triumph Mayflower that neatly complemented her jacket, skirt and nylons.

'Back in the good old days of public executions,' I continued, 'when Jack Ketch was dangling felons from Tyburn Tree, the Mob would regularly break out into the most glorious displays of drinking and fighting and, most especially, fornicating.'

'Eeh, I never knew that,' she said, opening the front door onto the suitably funereal rain lashing the street. 'Sounds indecent.' She opened a large umbrella and, shielding my path to the car, thrillingly hooked her arm through mine. Her red nails were bright as winter berries against the sober cloth of my coat.

'Indecent is just the word,' I said, clambering into the back of the car. 'It's the wonderful notion, you see, that *one is not yet inside the box oneself* that creates an unnatural and naughty high.'

'Not sure about that, Mr Box,' said Miss Beveridge, stuttering the car into life. 'Last spring, we sent me Nan up the crematorium chimney and had to spend a good half-hour brushing her off our Gannexes.'

I laughed. Miss Beveridge was a find. Her eyes crinkled in the narrow reflection of the driving mirror.

She turned the car round and we sliced through the puddles onto Whitehall, the view through the windscreen peppered with pollen and smeared into greasy triangles by the action of the wipers.

The journey took us about half an hour, by which time the rain was thudding down onto the cemetery's broad-leafed horse-chestnuts and running off the noses of weeping angels, making them look clammy as wet clay.

I got out of the car, straightened the Windsor knot on my tie and set off, the girl holding the umbrella over us. Many of the graves we passed were neglected, their stone borders breached, grisly green marble chippings spilling out onto the muddy path. Dead flowers had been stuffed into wire dustbins.

I stopped briefly as I spotted a grand building standing at the centre of a confluence of pathways. It was an old, black-doored chapel, filthy with age – and I realised with a start that I'd once, long ago, driven a hansom cab into it. That was during the complicated business of the Vesuvius Club when Christopher Miracle and I had both been young . . .

Oh, poor Christopher.

There were only a handful of brolly-bearing mourners grouped around the churned-up red earth, their wizened faces rendered blank and emotionless by the surfeit of burying that comes with old age. I nodded to acquaintances, fellow survivors of a shattered generation. Unbidden, images flickered through my mind. That first meeting with Miracle at one of Maudie Risborough's Chelsea crushes back in the Naughty Nineties. I was the ingénu dauber, pale, skinny, almost innocent. Miracle was the lionised portraitist, glowing, strapping, beautiful. He could have demolished me and my fragile reputation with a single gesture or a well-placed *bon mot*. But he'd shown me such kindness that dizzying afternoon that we'd soon become firm friends.

Not quite as firm as I would have liked, alas, but then Miracle had never shared my egalitarian proclivities. Occasional flashes of his startlingly classical physique in the Wigmore Street steam rooms had had to suffice until Time (and regular encounters with a priapic Scots guardsman on Rotten Row) had cured me of the pash.

Then, shortly after I'd frustrated the insane schemes of Victoria Wine and her deadly manservant Oddbins, Miracle had finally cottoned on to my by-line in espionage. I'd been forced to tell him all about the Royal Academy and my scandalous adventures – after which, sometimes unwillingly, he'd assisted me on many a hair-raising adventure – as you might recall from *The Case of the Insecure Syrup*.

Then had come the Great War, the Franco-Swiss mission to Lit-de-Diable and the injuries from which that wonderful blond boy had never wholly recovered. Miracle had drifted through his money and the years, never quite committing to anything. When last I'd seen him he'd just taken over – in a desultory fashion – a business that manufactured fruit cordial. Then it had all come to an abrupt end with Miracle's Jaguar XK 120 tearing wildly through the streets of Cape Town before plunging into the Atlantic.

Whatever could have made him do it?

I looked down at the yawning, saturated grave as though it might provide answers. The rain thudded off the oak and the brass tablet bearing my friend's name.

'*Requiescat in pace*,' I murmured.

I supposed that investigating Miracle's demise would bring my career neatly, if depressingly, full circle.

An unnecessarily ginger vicar droned through the usual eulogies and then clapped shut the soggy pages of his Bible. I tossed a posy of flowers into the grave: crimson roses for mourning, violets for modesty, sunflowers for loyalty and baby's breath for love everlasting. Propped against a nearby headstone was a rather ugly arrangement of blooms, done up into the shape of a bottle of squash. The 'M' for 'Miracle' trademark had been picked out in poppies.

I noticed my gloves were smeared with wet mud but Miss Beveridge was there in an instant, proffering a clean handkerchief. As I rubbed at the red stain, my gaze met that of a very fat man I'd not seen previously.

He was perhaps seventy years, plum-purple, chewing rather noisily on something or other and regarding his fellow mourners with what I can only describe as a sort of amused contempt. The features were somehow familiar and I realised, as Miss Beveridge and I left the graveside, that this must be Miracle's brother, Quintin. Although we had only met once or twice, I felt compelled to offer the usual sentiments. The girl and I fell into step with him as he ambled towards the gated exit.

'Mr Miracle?'

He turned a smiling moon-face towards me. 'I am he.'

Nodding to Miss Beveridge, he gestured towards the inscription on a nearby headstone that had almost disappeared under slick, dark ivy. '"Only sleeping",' he read aloud. 'God, what a thought! What would we do if the buggers woke up, eh?' He plunged his hand into his pocket. 'Can I tempt you with a liquorice comfit?'

'Thank you, no,' I said.

'My dear?' he offered.

Miss Beveridge shook her head. 'No, ta.'

'I don't know if you remember me,' I said. 'My name's Lucifer Box.' Liquid mud squelched onto my black shoes. 'I was a friend of Christopher.'

'I'm afraid I must get on—'

'I wonder if I could speak to you', I said quickly. 'In private?'

He looked about, as though hoping for a better offer. Then, shrugging, he said, 'Very well. It's slackening off,' he noted, holding out a gloved hand and peering at the heavens. 'Shall we sit?'

We made our way to a grim little shelter, larded all over in municipal green paint. Here and there, the metal had erupted into rusty pustules like on the legs of a pier. Miss Beveridge stood dutifully to one side and shook the droplets from her umbrella.

Quintin Miracle eased himself onto the bench and stared happily into space, chewing like a cow with its cud. His piggy eyes twinkled mischievously and his hand darted into his trousers. 'How about an Allsort?'

Again I demurred.

He made a happy little noise. 'Your loss, chum. Though, *entre nous*, I'm not so keen on the coconut ones. If I had my way, they'd do away with them and just have more liquorice. Lovely black liquorice. Shiny as a beetle's back. The world could stand more liquorice, don't you think, Mr . . . ?'

'Box.'

'Box, yes. I remember you now.'

'I'd like to speak to you about your brother,' I said.

'Would you indeed? I shall get his lolly,' he said abruptly.

With distaste, I realised that this was not some fresh obsession centred around Wall's ice cream. 'Oh?'

'Yes. I've seen the will. Oodles of cash. I've always fancied opening a little sweetie shop.'

'Mr Miracle—'

'Well, I say sweeties. I mean liquorice, obviously. Can't get enough of the stuff. If I had my way it wouldn't be so damned small. Imagine! A sherbet fountain as big as a golf-bag! I can afford it now.'

Miss Beveridge glanced across at me and rolled her eyes.

I decided to try another tack. 'Where do you stand on the Pomfret Cake?'

Quintin's face lit up. 'Ah! A connoisseur! *Charmant!*' The fat hand nipped into the sweet packet again, retrieving a treasure trove of colourful Allsorts, along with assorted bus tickets and fragments of tobacco. All ended up crammed into his mouth. 'Old Norman.'

'Who?'

'Pomfret. Old Norman for Pontefract. Where the cakes come from. *Entre nous*,' he repeated, then winked slyly, as though sharing a great confidence, 'they're a bit on the insubstantial side for my tastes. But, like the bootlace, they have their charms. Now, what was it you wanted to know?'

'Your brother—'

'Well, we were never close,' he sighed. 'But it's very sad and all. I remember when we were boys, Papa took us on an outing to the Bassett's factory in Sheffield. Such delights! Pipes, tablets, Blackjacks—'

'Can you think of any reason why he would have wanted to take his own life?'

'The business with the motor car, you mean? None at all.' He smiled and his teeth were streaked yellow-black. 'Though he was never the same after the Somme, you know.'

I looked down, sadly. 'Yes, I do know.'

'Poor old Chris. Always had the looks, of course. Mama's golden boy.' Was there a trace of bitterness in the younger Miracle's tone? 'Suppose he just couldn't face it.'

'Face what?'

'Getting decrepit and ugly. But what's the alternative, eh? That's what I always say. For myself, I've embraced it! Quite like being a smelly old gargoyle. Takes time to cultivate a tum like this!'

He patted his belly and cackled so hugely that remnants of rain shivered from the awning of the shelter onto the concrete.

'Funny thing is,' he continued, 'he'd seemed so much more full of life lately. Got quite interested in his business. Though why choose ruddy ginger pop, or whatever it is, of all things? I mean, I tried to convince him otherwise. Plenty of attractive alternatives, what?'

'Liquorice?' I asked innocently.

'Naturally! There was a prime site for sale near York—'

'Yes,' I drawled. 'Remarkable lack of foresight on his part.'

Quintin wiped a dewdrop from his red nose. 'Mind you, that hadn't been going so well of late. The squash lark.'

'No?'

'No. Some sort of boardroom battle. A take-over bid.'

'Really?' I asked, intrigued. 'By whom?'

'Search me,' said Quintin, winding a liquorice bootlace round his fat finger and nibbling on the end. 'Last letter I got from Chris mentioned it. He sounded a bit down in the dumps. They were offering more and more loot but he didn't want to sell. Shareholders thought differently. Perhaps that explains why he did . . . what he did.'

'Perhaps. Though he never seemed the type.'

'Type?'

'To take his own life.'

Miracle's brother grunted. 'Well, Mr Box, I suppose they never do.'

I rose and smoothed down my trousers. 'Thanks very much for your time. And again, my condolences.'

He nodded, smiled childishly, looking out over the dripping graveyard. 'Imagine! A sherbet fountain as big as a golf-bag!'

Miss Beveridge was standing a little way off. I joined her and we walked towards the car.

'Find out what you wanted, sir?' she asked.

'Not really.' I shrugged. 'Perhaps I'm reading too much into my friend's death. This was very kind of you, by the way. Bringing me here.'

'Not at all, Mr Box.'

'Please,' I said. 'Call me Lucifer.'

Miss Beveridge flushed slightly. 'Oh no, sir. Couldn't possibly do that.'

'Why ever not?'

'Wouldn't be right, sir. I mean . . . you being who you are and all.'

I laughed and adjusted my damp hat. That tingling anticipation was rising within me again. 'I was recently complaining to Mr Playfair that I have no wish to become venerable. What's your name? Christian name, I mean?'

'Coral.'

I stopped and held out my hand. 'Hello, Coral.'

She gave a nervous laugh and shook it. ''Ello . . . Lucifer.'

'See?' I said, walking on. 'That wasn't so hard, was it? Now then, my glittering career. Where had we got to?'

Coral Beveridge's face became suddenly animated, like a child asking for her favourite bedtime story. 'Dr Fetch! Dr Fetch!' she said excitedly.

'Ah, now you're talking. Dr Cassivelaunus Fetch. The Man with the Celluloid Hand. He formed A.C.R.O.N.I.M. around the turn of the century – when I was in my full vigour and you, my dear Coral, were no more than the first gleam of a twinkle. Fetch and I crossed swords many a time back in the good old days.'

'How did he lose the 'and?' she asked wonderingly.

I chuckled. 'I can laugh about it now, although it was rather serious at the time. Fetch dressed himself up as a woman and infiltrated the Suffragist movement. His intention was to go one better than Mrs Pankhurst and throw a *horse* under the *King*.'

'Flippin' 'eck!'

'Audacious scheme. Would have worked but . . .'

'But for you, sir.'

'*Lucifer*.'

Miss Beveridge acknowledged my gentle rebuke with a nod. I smiled. 'My God. I haven't thought about Fetch in years.'

'You almost sound as if you miss him,' she noted.

'Perhaps I do. Those were glorious days. Best of my life, really.'

I shivered, though not through cold, feeling glad to put the cemetery behind me. We had reached the car and Miss Beveridge held open the door for me. 'Now then,' I murmured, placing a gloved hand over hers. 'How about that lunch?'

She looked at my hand on hers and said: 'Oh!'

Then she glanced down quickly at her shoes. 'No . . . no, thank you, sir. I mean . . . I think I'd better be getting home.'

I withdrew my hand as though scorched. 'Coral, I'm so sorry. I thought that perhaps you and I . . .'

And now she looked me full in the face and laughed. The

delicious tingle of anticipation began to disperse. My face fell. 'I thought you might be keen to, you know . . . You seemed as if you might want to . . .'

'Oh, I'm right keen on that!' she blurted out. 'But you're too old for me, sir. I like a nice firm cock, me.'

.5.
BLOOD ORANGE

By the evening, the rain had stopped. The muggy atmosphere, however, remained. Somewhat deflated by Miss Beveridge's brutal assessment, I returned to Downing Street to plan a night of oblivion.

Rank has its privileges. Long-time readers may be pleased and a little relieved to know that, after a lifetime of penury, my elevation to the post of 'Joshua Reynolds' had brought with it a juicy stipend. This, combined with a renewed interest in the painters of the turn of the century, had finally allowed me to spruce up Number Nine to my satisfaction. Well, *I* didn't spruce it up, of course, but rather employed a battery of truculent youths in blue overalls to do it for me. Whilst I sat in happy contemplation, lads with oily hair and big boots happily clod-hopped over the dust-sheets, slurping at treacly tea and giving me the occasional devastatingly proletarian smile. One or two had even been persuaded to pose for me and – oh, their terrible beauty! Wondrously surly versions of Sargent's *Madame X*, draping the looped straps of their overalls off bare, creamy shoulders.

But there was no one waiting for me in Downing Street now. I had planned to bathe and change but instead, restless and out of sorts, I decided to drive the Bentley up to Town.

Soho thrummed like a wire across a drum – reeking of camphor from summer clothes, with the sizzle of neon café signs and the scents of expectation: tobacco, coffee, sweat, sex. Wide-open restaurant doors belched Bolognese over the smell of the drains and tarmac.

I zipped past Little Italy and swung right into Dean Street. A youth in a bum-freezer absently sloshed a pail of soapy water across the pavement, forming a black bloodstain. His hair shone with Brylcreem and a desperate moustache clung to his lip like an anemone to a wet rock.

I slowed down in the traffic. He caught my eye and, clearly having finished his shift, wandered over. 'Peps?' he offered, laying an elbow on the sill of the open car window. 'Weed? Bennies? Barbs?'

'How thrilling of you to offer,' I said. 'However, I think I can struggle through the evening without artificial stimulants. Thanks all the same.'

The youth just shrugged and shambled away from the Bentley towards a pale blue moped that was parked on the kerb. He kick-started it and the engine rattled and fired. Where was he off to, I wondered. Pockets stuffed with cheap fags, pills and French letters, roaring through the sultry night . . .

The traffic shifted and I headed north towards Oxford Street, passing narrow entranceways as quaint as Eastbourne beach huts. In most, below stuttering red lamps, hovered ghostly whores. Out of the tail of my eye, I caught the slash of pink blouse and pink mouth, stockings with holes in them the size of two-bob bits, cheaply peroxided hair tumbling out of bent pins. As I drove by, the girls drifted in and out like figures on a weather house, and fugitive memories sprang up unbidden. How gaily I had trawled these same streets as a young man, a raffish De Quincy, my scarlet-lined opera cloak shielding each of my couplings as completely as the veil of the night itself.

The car was idling again. I glanced over my shoulder and the image thrown back in a tobacconist's window – an old man hunched over a steering wheel – banished all such nostalgia.

Then another memory intruded. An occasion, a lifetime ago, when wee me, dressed in a little sailor-suit, had been ushered into the presence of a dying aunt. She was a vision in black bombazine, extending a fragile hand from the dark pit of her bath chair to stroke my smooth cheek. 'Ah,' she had cooed, 'little Lucifer. How I wish I could change places with you . . .'

Now, in the plate-glass reflection I seemed to see myself stretching out a withered claw to touch the face of youth with envy, envy, envy . . .

I shook my head. Christ! I was being ridiculous! I'd never been a maudlin soul and had no intention of starting now. Throwing the car briskly into first, I dodged the traffic of Oxford Street and headed for the fabled *Blood Orange.*

Three storeys tall, the club staggered between a pair of more respectable buildings like a drunk between two coppers, the windows of its tumbledown, mucky Queen Anne façade bobbing with shadows and candlelight. In its twenties heyday, it had been the epitome of glamour. Now, in its dotage, it had a seedy appeal all its own. I parked the car in a cobbled mews that stank of last night's relief, then went up worn steps into a kind of vestibule.

A bare bulb caked in dust threw ugly shapes over the chocolate-brown walls and the fretwork of a tiny, asthmatic lift. With a melancholy sigh, cables twisting and coiling like the undulations of a charmed cobra, the lift arrived with a jarring thump. I pulled open the grille, got in, and jabbed at the soiled green button, which had seen too many thumbs.

The lift juddered upwards two floors and then decanted me into a big, dark room, every available surface covered with shards of broken mirror, grotesquely reflecting the heaving mass of jabbering, laughing faces. A shifting miasma of tobacco smoke rolled under the low ceiling like a storm cloud.

I intended to get very drunk.

I headed for the curved bar, where sat a big man with a neck like a block of ice cream. He was forcing flat champagne onto a sad-eyed girl in her mother's furs, whilst two skinny queens in evening dress hooted at each other, their wolfish features shattered, split and reflected in the mirrored walls. Incongruously, a teenage Boy Scout (I couldn't seem to get away from them at present) was wandering from table to table with a collecting tin. A gross, red-eared fellow, like an ogre in a fairy tale, slipped a coin into the tin and then waved the lad away.

There was a loud bellowing laugh and the man at the bar slumped to the floor, one shoe off, his threadbare sock wet through.

I knew them all. Loved and loathed the pack of them. Such was the *Blood Orange*.

However, at one of the two dozen tables, sat a stranger; an insignificant-looking bald man with little puffs of white hair sprouting from behind each ear. His white silk scarf had twisted up the points of his collar to give him a Pickwickian air.

Although I didn't recognise him as an habitué of the club, his face was nevertheless oddly familiar.

Leaning like a question mark against the wall right by him was a young man of Negroid appearance, though pale for one of his race. Toreador-slim in skinny suit and tie, his glossy black hair was cut in a straight fringe, and acid-green socks showed above pointy shoes.

He watched the Pickwickian from under sleepy eyelids.

Dismissing them both from my mind, I made my way to the bar where stood, presiding over this whole carnival of damnation, a colossal female in canary yellow. At that very moment, she was knocking back a pint of Dog's Nose and pulling a flap of skirt out of the cheeks of her buttocks.

My dear servant Delilah was now as old as the hills and as white-haired as I. But age had not withered her, nor custom made stale anything but the irrepressible reek from her armpits. We'd been through a hell of a lot together, and when fortune had finally come my way, in a mood of sudden philanthropy, I had granted her freedom from domestic service. With her savings, she had bought the leasehold on the crumbling *Blood Orange*, and the rest, as they say, is hysteria.

'A brandy and soda, my good woman,' I demanded, sneaking up behind her and giving her a playful punch on the arm.

The old bruiser span round, fist raised, a mad-dog gleam in her eyes. Her mouth was smeared with lipstick and had the appearance of an open sore. 'Mr Box! Mr Box, sir!' she cackled, enfolding me in her immensity. 'What a sight for sore 'uns! Cor, I nearly felled ya there. Get sat down and I'll fetch you some plonk.' She propelled me towards a splintering stool.

'How's business?' I enquired as she sloshed cognac into a none-too-clean tumbler and slid it over the tarnished veneer towards me.

'Same as ever,' she growled. 'I gotta read the riot act three times a week just to keep the buggers in order but they're not a bad lot. And they know not to fight too 'ard or they'll get a taste of *this*.' She bared her meaty fist from which sprouted wiry grey hairs. 'Mind you,' she continued, 'some might say as we've gawn up in the world.'

'How so?'

She nodded towards the fluffy-haired Pickwick-like fellow I'd noticed earlier. The coloured youth was now sitting with him and they seemed to be having a fairly lively conversation. The older man was looking nervously about and nibbling at his fingernails. The boy was shaking his head, ever so slightly, and the dead straight hair shifted like a curtain over his smooth forehead. 'Know who that is?' asked Delilah, with a wink.

I frowned. 'The boy?'

'Nah, nah, nah. Dunno about him. The old geezer.'

'I feel I should,' I admitted. 'He's certainly familiar. But I'm not as good with faces as once I was.'

'Sir Vyvyan Hooplah,' breathed Delilah, rubbing a soiled tea-towel around a gin glass. 'Remember him?'

'I do!' I whispered. 'Yes, of course. Used to be . . . Secretary of State for – no – he was Head of the Board of Health, wasn't he? Under Asquith!'

Delilah shrugged hugely. 'I just remember him from the picture papers. Nearly got the top job, didn't he?'

I nodded, intrigued. 'Yes. He did.' And indeed, it was Hooplah. Pinched and mean-spirited by reputation, he was a pillar, supporting wall and front porch of the Establishment. And yet there he was, sat at one of Delilah's chipped tables – apparently in search of oblivion, like me.

It was hard to make out details as the packed club's clientele swirled around in my line of sight but I saw the Negroid youth gesticulating and Hooplah angrily pushing him away. Then the scene disappeared as the room was plunged into darkness. A spotlight hit the tiny bandstand and couples staggered into drunken dancing.

'And what you been up to, sir?' asked Delilah, a mischievous twinkle in her bloodshot orbits. 'Helping some kiddies across the road? Opening a new 'ospital ward? Or have you been going to the park to chuck Hovis at the ducks?'

'Now, now, Delilah,' I said, sipping gingerly at the brandy. 'You're sounding petulant again.'

'Well,' she drawled, 'not like the bloody old days, is it? Stuck behind a desk fiddling with paper-clips. I bet you'd give a year of your life just for a nice juicy hassassination!'

I shook my head. 'Time to bring down the curtain, Delilah,' I said. 'The party's over.'

But scarcely had the words left my lips when I felt a sudden heat on my cheek, and my smeary glass exploded as a 9mm bullet slammed into the bar.

.6.
GOODBYE, PICCADILLY

I flung myself to the floorboards. Grit and dust choked me and the air was full of cordite. There was a shocked pause and then one of the stringy queens started screaming like a *castrato*.

In a ring of suddenly empty tables stood Sir Vyvyan Hooplah, brandishing a Luger. His ruddy face was suffused with a wicked grin and the clouds of hair behind his ears seemed to stand on end. He fired again, further fracturing the mirrored walls. The exotic-looking young man shielded his head with long, slim fingers.

Delilah reacted with the speed of a panther. A long-in-the-tooth panther, mind you, but still fairly nippy. As I scrambled to my feet, she rolled up her sleeves and prepared to give Hooplah what for.

'Look out! Look out!' cackled Sir Vyvyan delightedly, loosing off another shot. 'I'll take on the lot of you, d'you hear? Haha!' His face was now almost violet above the white scarf. 'Never fired a weapon, d'you see? Sat out the war on my silly old rump. Both wars, in point of fact, but now . . . *Now!*'

'All right, mate,' warned Delilah, approaching stealthily. 'Time you turned in.'

'Not likely!' yelled the berserk former politician.

He fired another bullet and then proceeded to propel himself head-first through the crowd. The Negroid boy reached out and got him by the ankles but the old buffer slid from his grasp and clattered to the floor. Then Hooplah righted himself, galloped towards the lift, dragged back the grille and turned to face the room, a manic glitter in his eyes. 'See? See!' he roared. 'I'm a match for you!'

The Luger spat fire into the smoky air and the great central chandelier splintered, smashing crystal droplets to the floor like frozen tears.

The lift chugged into life and Hooplah was gone.

'Stairs!' I cried. 'Get to the stairs!'

Delilah and I tore from the room and onto the *Blood Orange*'s ill-lit stairwell. We clattered down two flights, flung open the front door and dashed outside, only to be greeted by the roar of an engine and a great screech of tyres. Two sharp reports, a blur of scarlet and Hooplah was off, careering wildly around parked motors, accelerating south towards Oxford Street.

I gaped at Delilah. 'He's stolen my ruddy car!'

Delilah heaved a huge sigh, shoulders sagging in defeat. 'Come on then. I'll call the rozzers.'

'What are you talking about?' I bristled. 'I want my Bentley back!'

'Yeah, but—'

I looked round swiftly and my heart leaped as I caught sight of the ugly young moped driver who'd earlier offered me stimulants. 'I thought you wanted to recapture the halcyon days, you old fossil,' I cried to Delilah. 'Come on!'

We dashed the few yards to the moped, our hips clicking like knitting needles. The youth, now chatting up a girl in bright yellow pedal-pushers, looked at me, his black brows contracting as I placed a hand on his machine. 'Awfully sorry,' I smiled disarmingly, 'but that old bugger's pinched my car. Hope you don't mind but I've got to get it back.'

A strand of his Brylcreemed hair flopped forward, almost poking him in the eye. 'So?' he drawled, winking at the girl. 'What's that got to do with me?'

'Not a lot,' I admitted calmly and, stepping to one side, allowed Delilah's chunky fist to connect with his chin.

''Ere!' piped up the girl in the pedal-pushers. With a mildly surprised grunt, her beau slid from the moped's seat. Delilah caught him deftly, then, with only a little difficulty, dragged him onto the pavement. A groan of effort, and I swung my leg across the broad back of the moped. Behind me, Delilah did likewise and the poor vehicle sagged under the weight. I chugged the engine into life and, belching fumes, we screeched off into the traffic in pursuit of my Bentley.

'What the hell can have got into the old fool?' I yelled as we gathered speed.

'I ain't never seen him in the club before,' cried Delilah. In one of the huge mirrors clamped to each handlebar, I saw her wiping sweat from her brick-like forehead. 'He just wandered in looking a bit nervy-like.'

I peered ahead at the silvery car bumpers as we shot across Oxford Street and back into Soho. 'Maybe he's cracked,' continued Delilah. 'Pressure of work.'

I shook my head. 'No, no. He's been retired for years. In any case—'

A fugitive memory began to intrude on me, like a trapped bee knocking against a window casement. 'Do you know, Delilah, this is— *Look out!*'

I swerved, careering past a leggy girl in lethal heels. Poland Street shot past like a dimly lit canyon. The warm air whipped at my face and my hair streamed back off my forehead in snowy fronds. Ahead, manoeuvring through the traffic with terrifying disregard, was the Bentley. I winced as Hooplah pranged a black cab, eliciting an explosion of horn parping, and a stream of oaths from its cloth-capped driver, as he scraped against the chassis. A youth in corduroys yelped in terror as the Bentley mounted the kerb and, scattering pedestrians like skittles, skidded off.

'The lunatic,' I muttered. 'He'll top someone.' I swung us right in hot pursuit. 'And Christ knows what he's doing to my suspension!'

'What was you gonna say?' cried Delilah.

I crouched low over the handlebars. 'Tell you later!'

Ahead tail-lights blurred, speckled with the amber signs of black cabs. There was a fanfare of protesting horns as Hooplah smashed into Berwick Street. A mass of gabardined punters fled as the car screamed past them. Then, suddenly, dozens of covered market stalls blocked his way.

Hooplah slammed on the Bentley's brakes. I could see the top of his bald head shining in the electric light as he considered his next move. In an instant he had revved the engine and the car leapfrogged forward, ploughing into the stalls and sending shattered planks, fruit and vegetables spuming into the air. As we gave chase, a fat cauliflower smacked Delilah on the side of the head and, without warning, she bounced off the back of the moped. It bucked upwards at once and I struggled to keep control.

There was a sickening crunch as Hooplah sliced my beloved Bentley through the last of the stalls and, in a plume of exhaust smoke, zig-zagged towards Shaftesbury Avenue.

Righting myself, I threw a glance over my shoulder to see Delilah struggling to her feet. Relieved, I pressed on, accelerating past the arched naughtiness of the Revue Bar – furtive tarts diving for their lives – then weaving down Rupert Street before bucking onto Shaftesbury Avenue in hot pursuit.

As I stuttered through the traffic, I peered ahead, desperate to catch a glimpse of the Bentley's red livery. And yes – at last – there it was! Hemmed in and unable to proceed. To my horror, Hooplah was relentlessly ramming the back bumper of the car in front. Still perched atop the stolen moped, I zipped past an overheating sports car until I was just behind the crazed former Cabinet Minister. 'Hooplah!' I hollered. 'Stop the damned car! What the hell—'

He turned and the look on his ancient face fairly made my blood run cold. There was an intensity, a sort of mania in the eyes, which utterly transformed him.

'Oh hello!' he cackled, spittle dribbling onto his chin. 'Haha! Hello, old man! Old man! Haha! That's good!'

I tried to inch the moped forward but a determined old family tourer was blocking my way.

'Hooplah!' I cried desperately. 'Sir Vyvyan! Get out of the car before you kill someone!'

'Get out? Get *out*?' The response came as a choked whisper. 'Are you quite mad?' Suddenly the gun was in his hand again and he loosed off a couple of shots into the air. I ducked down.

'I must get on!' whooped Hooplah. 'No time to lose! Can't you see? Can't you see what's happened? It's a bloody miracle!'

At last, the other car crawled out of the way and I was able to pull level with the Bentley. Hooplah aimed the Luger right at me but I managed to knock it away and reach out to grab his collar. Then I almost toppled over as the light switched from red to amber, the traffic ahead suddenly moved and the old lunatic slammed the car into gear, rocketing off once again.

I swore under my breath, righted myself and squeezed the handle of the moped. It chugged forward but then the bloody thing stalled. Precious moments were wasted as I kick-kick-kicked at the starting pedal. Then I was once more giving chase.

Still, that nagging memory persisted. There was something about Hooplah's behaviour. Something familiar . . .

Suddenly, a stretch of clear road opened, leading, with dreadful inevitability, to the statue of Eros. Hooplah took immediate advantage and opened up the Bentley's throttle, weaving across the road and tattooing the asphalt with streaks of burned rubber. Cursing the sluggish moped, I urged it on, leaning forward heavily against the handlebars, batting aside the insects that zipped into my eyes and mouth.

I could hear the Bentley's outraged engine even above the din of the night-time traffic, and glimpsed Hooplah's head twisting round, the glint of his teeth as he giggled insanely. Then the Bentley was powering past everything in sight, zooming down the very centre of the road. Hooplah attempted a right turn and suddenly the car was on two wheels, smacking onto the pavement and heading for the famous statue. In a blur, the motor flipped over and slammed sidelong into Eros with a devastating percussion. The Bentley's windscreen erupted outwards, and Hooplah was hurled onto the steps beneath the aluminium statue. As though in sympathy, Eros sagged as the masonry crumbled beneath him, arrow now aimed downwards, as if to pierce the old man's heart.

I screeched to a halt, swung my legs over the moped and stumbled towards the scene of the accident. A gawping crowd had already gathered around Hooplah and the Bentley. I fought my way through the mass of sequins, duffel coats and crumpled uniforms towards the politician. The Bentley lay in a heaped pile, steam hissing from the ruined chassis, oil pooling from her mortal wound.

A thin trickle of blood was dribbling from Hooplah's lips onto the starched ends of his wing-collar.

'Sir Vyvyan?' I whispered urgently. 'Sir Vyvyan, can you hear me?'

His eyes fluttered open, startlingly bright amidst the gore that smeared his features.

'Wonderful!' he murmured. 'Wonderful!'

I pressed my face closer to his. 'What happened to you?'

His eyes began to close.

'Hooplah!' I cried. *'For God's sake, what happened?'*

The old fellow began to chuckle gently and, struggling to get his breath, whispered, '*Le . . . le papillon noir . . .*'

I frowned. 'What?'

But Hooplah's eyes had closed. A broad smile spread over his blood-soaked face – and he was gone.

From close by I heard the clang of a police bell and looked up. To my surprise, in amongst the ogling crowd was the coloured boy from the *Blood Orange*. Girl-slim, fingers bright with rings, he gazed at me from behind the geometrically straight fall of his black hair. Then he was gone, melting into the crowd.

My instincts told me that he was involved in all this. Hooplah had seemed perfectly normal until he started talking to that young man. I moved swiftly after him and was almost knocked down by a wheezing Delilah who had finally caught up.

'Christ,' she gasped, 'I should be careful what I wish for. I ain't got the strength for this lark any more. What 'appened?'

'Dead,' I muttered.

Delilah shook her massive head. 'Bloody odd. Never seen anyone act like that before.'

I clambered onto the moped and kick-started it into life once more. 'I have.'

.7.
TICK-TOCK

Travel, though it broadens the mind, narrows life expectancy. The positive benefits of each lovely foreign vista, every restful *felucca* sail down the blue Nile, are offset by the hateful tyranny of actually getting there. The cramped train, the soulless airport, the dreadful people and, perhaps worst of all, *carrying one's own luggage*. Whatever became of bearers?

Athens Airport wore the familiar, bleary look of a late night arrival, stale with sweat and tobacco. A handful of uniformed officials shuffled about the shoddy buildings, staring sullenly at us newcomers. A shoe-shine man in a too-heavy topcoat waited expectantly by the exit, grinning like a simpleton. I was keeping the Negroid youth in sight. He was some way behind me, head buried in a well-thumbed paperback. I angled my hat low over my eyes, hoping to blend in. He'd leaped into a cab at Piccadilly, which I'd followed all the way to London Airport. Abandoning the moped, I'd quickly ascertained that the boy was taking a plane to Athens and promptly booked myself onto the same flight. I'd been lucky and had studiously managed to avoid him as we boarded, and then, much later, disembarked.

All at once, I was being ushered to the passport booth, its glass façade smudged with fingermarks. I handed over the comfortingly solid navy book, the Britannia emblem shining like iron pyrite in the ghastly neon glare.

A scowling official looked me up and down, scratching at his scarcely shaven chin. 'How long you here?'

'Fortnight,' I lied.

'Business or pleasure?'

'Oh, pleasure. Always pleasure. And, for the record, I think you should have your marbles back.'

He grunted, licked the rubber stamp and thumped it heavily onto a virgin page of the passport. Waving me through, he turned his attention to a skinny Welsh couple shivering in shorts and wind-cheaters. The boy was some way behind them and still hadn't looked my way.

I quickly exited. Outside, the air was sharp, the darkening sky cobalt as a ceramic tile and crammed with stars. I lit a cigarette, hailed a cab and then sat in the back, ignoring the jabbering driver as I waited for the mysterious youth to emerge.

At last he did so, shouldering his bag and getting into a cab of his own. We followed him through cramped, dingy streets overhung with sagging cables, like stitches on burst wounds, until he reached the dimly lit railway station. A big, elderly-looking train was already at the platform, huffing as though impatient. I checked the departures board. The train was heading for Istanbul. In five minutes.

The slender youth swung open a door, took a swift look around, and then disappeared inside the train. I paid off my driver and then raced to the telegraph office. I just had time to rattle off a wire. I knew of someone in Istanbul who might prove very useful . . .

With moments to spare, I pulled myself up onto the train, feeling a little thrill of anticipation as I settled down into a private cabin. The engine lurched, the giant wheels squealed and the journey east began.

The cabin was small but well ordered, the woodwork a pleasant amber-brown. When the conductor came, I paid for my ticket in sterling and ordered up a bottle of schnapps before stripping off my wilted linen suit. I'd have to buy myself a whole new wardrobe once we reached Turkey. What a happy thought!

The booze was harsh but acceptable. I got into bed – the cotton sheets wonderfully cool – and let the thoughts that were buzzing inside my head settle into some kind of order.

As I'd remarked to Delilah, the crazed behaviour of Sir Vyvyan Hooplah was not entirely unfamiliar to me. Bells had rung. Distant ones, but they'd rung all the same. Recently, I'd noticed other incidents bearing marked similarities.

Just twelve months ago, Sir Douglas Gobetween, another former Cabinet Minister, had broken his neck after falling out of an apple tree. When questioned about his behaviour, his grieving wife could only say that he'd woken up that morning determined to 'go scrumping'. Then there'd been Baroness Watchbell, the elderly pharmacist who, not long after Gobetween's demise, had strapped herself to the wing of a Cessna Bobcat and collided with a mountain. Then there was Père Meddler, the French cleric, whose work on the immune system had brought him the Nobel Prize. Happily celibate for years, he had suddenly, at the age of eighty, taken himself off to Marrakech and died in a fit of sexual excess involving thirty-eight boys and a Barbary macaque. The question was, had these silly old buffers just got it into their heads to have one last hurrah before the graveyard – or their deaths connected? And was Christopher so-called suicide part of the same, bizarre pattern?

And then there were Hooplah's dying words. '*Le papillon noir*'. The Black Butterfly.

I knew this was the French term for depression. Had Hooplah gone off his rocker because he'd been clinically depressed? At any rate, a curious picture was forming, made all the more strange by the presence, both at Hooplah's table and the scene of the accident, of the coloured youth. It wasn't much of a lead, but it was all I had.

The next day dawned hot and sunny. The great black engine, steam smothering its face like foam on the bridle of a mad horse, dragged us on. Station signs flashed past, unknown and dreadful in their loneliness.

I struggled back into the previous day's linen (such a horrid feeling, don't you think? – unless the reason for it is a saucy one) and then breakfasted in the dining car. A bored-looking waiter ministered to my needs, and then left me alone in the compartment. I turned an eye towards the dusty window, peering out at the excitingly impenetrable shadows of the dark forest blurring past. Sagging terracotta-tiled houses and crumbling churches flickered by like snapshots between the lush green of the pines, their faded oranges and cornflower-blues gay-seeming next to the brooding dark of the trees. I was reaching for my second coffee, when suddenly I became aware of another presence in the otherwise empty carriage.

He was standing by the door, willowy tall in a cut-throat-creased suit, black roll-neck sweater and sunglasses. The dead straight hair hung over his sunglasses.

'This seat taken?' he fluted. The accent was curious, faintly American.

I shook my head.

Without a word, my quarry slipped into the empty place and I felt his warm leg brush my knee. He didn't remove his sunglasses. In the blazing orange of the late-morning light, they glowed like moth's eyes. Then he smiled, showing perfect white teeth.

'Hi.'

'Hello,' I said quietly.

'Cigarette?' he asked.

'Thank you, no,' I said, patting my side. 'I have my own.'

He shook his head, ever so slightly, and the dead straight hair shifted over his smooth forehead. 'No, baby. I meant do you *have* a cigarette. For *me*?'

'Oh,' I said. 'Of course.' Reaching into my jacket, I produced my battered old silver case. He took out a Turkish mixture and held it gently between his long, slim fingers.

'Light?'

I felt in my pocket for a gas-lighter and managed to get a spark out of it. The flame leaped up and the youth closed both hands around mine as he leaned close to light his fag. He glanced up at me and there was a curious look in his hooded eyes. Pleasure? Mockery?

He blinked slowly again. 'Thanks.' As he withdrew his hands, his sleeve caught the polished coffee-pot, spilling it over the white cloth.

'Oh, man, I'm so sorry!' he said. 'Here, let me—'

'It's nothing. Don't bother.'

He shook his head, righted the pot and refilled my little cup. Then he sat back, smiling.

I lit a cigarette for myself and fixed the youth with a hard stare. 'Well, this is a pleasant surprise, Mr . . . ?'

He chuckled and the sound was curiously pretty, like the song of a bird. 'Names are very powerful things, baby. If you knew who I was, you might go telling tales out of school.'

'Now why ever would I want to do a thing like that?'

The boy shrugged, rumpling the shiny fabric of his beautifully cut suit. 'You might have taken exception to me.'

'The very idea. However, I have no qualms about introducing myself. My name's—'

'Oh, I know who *you* are,' he murmured.

'You do?'

'Uh-huh.'

He propped his elbows onto the table before us and rested his head on his hand. The long shadows threw his cheeks and jaw into relief, smooth as chocolate ice cream. Smoke from his cigarette drifted like a veil over his face. 'See, people have no respect these days,' he mused. 'Young people 'specially. They always wanna knock down everything that's gone before. I-con-o-clasm, they call it.'

'I am aware of the term,' I said.

The youth took a long drag. 'Even the good things, they wanna smash 'em up. I ain't like that. I appreciate history. Or heritage, you might say.'

'Rare in one so young,' I commented, tipping ash onto the saucer of my coffee cup.

He slid the sunglasses down the bridge of his nose, eyes glittering like Whitby jet beneath the sculpted hoods of their lids. 'Like I said, I know all about you, *Mr Lucifer Box*. You were good.'

'*Was* I?'

'You might even have been the very best. But there comes a time when you should retire from the field with some grace, baby. It just wouldn't be right for you to end it all . . . out here. Time's up. Tick-tock, baby. Tick-tock.'

He let his words hang in the air and turned back to the window, eyes flickering as he watched the landscape stream past.

I folded my arms. 'How kind of you to be concerned for my welfare. And for elucidating matters.'

'Huh?'

'Well, I wasn't sure whether I was on a wild-goose chase. Now I know I'm not.'

He threw back his head and giggled, slapping a long

brown hand against his chest. 'Good point. *Oops*.'

I felt a sudden warmth on my leg and realised with an electric thrill that he had slipped off his shoe and lain his bare foot against the flesh of my ankle. 'But listen, baby,' he cooed. 'Seriously – why don't you get off the train at the next station? Beautiful country around here. You could see the sights. Take it easy . . .'

His foot was moving slowly, lazily, up my calf, over my knee. 'Easy,' he breathed. 'Nice and easy . . .'

I felt his foot slide into my lap. Its heaviness and warmth were strangely wonderful. The boy gazed at me. 'But then you take the Orient Express or somesuch back home where you belong.' The pretty face suddenly hardened. 'This isn't work for old men.'

In an instant, my hand dived under the table and grabbed his ankle. With the other hand, I took hold of his big toe and bent it back savagely. He gasped in shock and pain and dropped his cigarette.

'And what exactly is this work of yours?' I cried.

'That'd be telling . . . wouldn't it?' he hissed between clenched teeth. 'Let go of me, you bastard!'

'Who *are* you?' I demanded.

He twisted in his seat and I jerked his toe back still further. He yelled, then scowled in fury. 'It'll take more than that to—'

'Name?' I insisted, jabbing my thumbnail into the soft flesh of the toe. 'NAME?'

'Kingdom!' he gasped at last. 'Kingdom Kum!'

I let his foot go at once and he pulled it back, like a whip.

'Damn you!' he cried. At once, he assumed a cross-legged position on the dusty seat and began rubbing at his naked foot. 'No call for *that*!'

I picked up my coffee and swirled it around the cup. It was thick as molasses. 'So, Kingdom – I may call you Kingdom, mayn't I? – it seems you know all about me but I know next to nothing about you. That strikes me as a very unfair arrangement.'

'Life's unfair, baby,' he snarled, massaging his bruised toe.

I fixed him with a level stare, blue eyes to brown. 'Really? How's yours been?'

He giggled, as though the whole incident was forgotten, and cocked his head to one side. 'Up and down.'

'And how does Sir Vyvyan Hooplah fit into it? You two were having a very animated chat last night in the *Blood Orange*.'

'Uh-huh.'

'Might I enquire what it was about?'

Kingdom Kum picked up his cigarette. It had burned a big brown hole in the tablecloth. 'Let me tell you a little story instead,' he whispered. 'Story about my daddy's boss. Mr Hyogo.'

I stubbed out my cigarette and made to get up. 'I don't have time for reminiscing—'

In a flash, there was a long, thin, deadly blade at my throat, bright against the white of his palm.

'On the other hand,' I gulped, 'you sound like a fascinating young fellow. Do go on.'

Kingdom Kum let the knife move slowly over my skin.

'Well, baby, Mr Hyogo, he used to slip into my sister's room some nights. My parents couldn't do anything about it for fear Daddy'd lose his job. But I did something about it. Eventually.'

'Oh yes?' I could feel the blade skimming my ill-shaved cheek.

'One night Mr Hyogo got between my sister's sheets but *she* wasn't there. *I* was. With this.' He inclined his wrist just a fraction and I could feel the pressure of the steel against the bone of my tensed jaw. 'Mr Hyogo didn't come again. In any sense of the word,' the youth told me. 'If you get my drift.'

I nodded.

'I could slit you open like a blowfish,' Kingdom Kum went on with deadly gravity. 'No one touches me,' he said. 'Not without my say-so.'

I swallowed and grinned foolishly. 'I have terrible manners. I always forget to ask nicely when I'm torturing people.'

The boy's face suddenly relaxed and he giggled again. The knife vanished up the expensively-cut sleeve as suddenly as it had appeared. 'Well, let's call this a warning, then,' he said lightly. 'A nice, friendly warning, Mr Lucifer Box.'

He rose like a wisp of smoke, and gave a graceful bow as he headed for the door. 'It's been an honour, sir. I mean that. But I do hope we shan't meet again. Next time, I might not be so friendly.' He waggled his hand and the light caught the watch on his slender wrist. 'Tick-tock, baby. Tick-tock.'

He pulled open the door, the noise of the rattling carriage increased for a second – and then he was gone.

There was a single, neat droplet of blood on the tablecloth. I touched a finger to my face and winced. Then I drank the last of my coffee with a suddenly less than firm hand.

.8.
THE MAN FROM 'STAMBOUL

I woke with a start and realised the train had stopped moving. Evening light washed into the cabin, staining the walls peach. Above the jug and basin on the lopsided washstand hung a cracked photograph of Attaturk – the face tinted with colour, slightly sinister in his severe black hat. The dying sun was slicing a dusty beam through a gap in the pale blue curtains.

I was fully dressed and hadn't even taken off my shoes. My mouth tasted as though something had crawled into it to die and there was a thudding pain behind my eyes. I knew the symptoms only too well. I'd been drugged!

Damn that boy. How had he done it? Could only have been the coffee. That textbook stunt, knocking over the pot. I cursed myself. I was getting too old for this. I'd learned precious little from him, other than his name – and that he was already acquainted with mine! At least my instincts had been right in one respect. Kingdom Kum *had* been involved in the bizarre death of Vyvyan Hooplah. However, I certainly had no intention of being scared off by his crude threats.

Istanbul announced itself with the achingly mournful call to prayer. I eased myself up off my bunk, scowled at the throbbing pain in my head and my sore cheek, and quickly left the train.

Of course, Kingdom Kum was long gone.

He could have been anywhere by now. Perhaps Istanbul was merely a staging-post for him. I could only hope that, if my contact in the city were half as good as his reputation promised, I could soon be back on Mr Kum's trail.

There was a reply waiting for me at the telegraph office, as I'd hoped, welcoming me to the city and giving the address of an hotel into which my contact had booked me.

I walked down from the station, the lemon-and-honey smoke that rose above the ancient city creating a bluish miasma. I lit a cigarette and took a moment or two to gaze out over the wonderful Bosphorus, alive with shipping on a fantastic scale. Trawlers, tankers, pleasure cruisers and yachts spangled the expanse of shimmering blue, rather like a Tudor map showing the arrangement of the Armada.

After a while, I found the hotel. It was one of those cosy places constructed in the old colonial style: a three-storey clapboard structure, painted an attractive green, the window frames outlined in white. Downstairs, all was cool and shadowy. A beaming concierge in a comical fez showed me to my room where I bathed, luxuriously, and surrendered my suit to be laundered. I put through a call to London and spent most of the afternoon shouting coded messages down the blower to Delilah. Of course, the old girl was officially retired, but she still had plenty of contacts amongst the 'Domestics' – the Academy's loyal staff of functionaries. Could they find a connection between those deaths: Gobetween, Watchbell, Meddler, Hooplah – and possibly Miracle? The crackly connection kept breaking, necessitating tedious journeys to the front desk. When I was done, I stretched out to sleep on the neat bed.

The night was very warm. Little blocks of charcoal burned brightly in swinging lamps outside shut-up shops, in which bejewelled scarves and mottled mirrors glinted. Here and there, a bundle of rags would suddenly stir into life and a swarthy face turn upwards, eyes glistening in the starlight. Clothes freshly laundered, I made my way up a stone stair and found myself on a raised concrete platform on which sprouted half a dozen cafés. Outside the first, a dervish was – well, *whirling* – for the benefit of giggling tourists, sprawled out on striped cushions. As they sucked on tall hookahs, a sickly-sweet aroma of apples and tobacco assailed me. I walked on until I came to the third café, parted a thin muslin curtain and went inside.

Formed from the intersection of a series of low arches, the room seemed to be the remains of some exquisite aqueduct, the brickwork still solid and dry, rough edges softened by cushions and fluttering drapes. The ceiling was so low, I had to stoop as I groped my way towards a hexagonal table.

A great rolling fug of tobacco smoke billowed overhead. The light sources were so discreet as to be almost negligible, just the odd red or blue lantern, throwing laughing faces into sharp silhouette, blurring the lines of lovers as they sank back into the downy embrace of the cushions.

A boy of about ten came wandering over as I sat. He was dressed in a plain white smock with an encrustation of paste jewels around the collar. I ordered a glass of coffee and the honey and nut sweetmeat *kadayif*. Both were utterly delicious, the coffee glutinous. Lighting a cigarette, I leaned back against the brickwork and let the scene wash over me. Lord, I'd missed Istanbul. I hadn't been there since the early days of the Franco-British Occupation, when a young man with a shy smile and tackle like a gorilla had kept me royally entertained. I had been tracking down the spy known only as Rosehip – the best belly-dancer in old 'Stamboul, who dusted her nipples with icing sugar in imitation of the snow-covered domes of the Topkapi. Happy days, happy days.

Glancing at my wristwatch, I turned as the muslin curtain parted and a huge man pushed his way inside. Interested heads turned his way as he barrelled forward, shoulders as broad as though he'd left the hanger inside his crumpled white suit. He plonked himself down at the table next to mine and barked at the boy to fetch him a pipe. The mosaic of light and deep shadow played over the contours of his huge head. He was like a bear in white linen, the swarthy face bisected by a drooping black moustache. Two gold rings sparkled in one ear. I noticed that the tip of the ear was ragged as though it had been bitten off. He glanced towards me and I saw that, though one eye gleamed darkly, the other was missing, replaced by a gold sovereign that had been screwed into the socket. It blazed briefly in the light, leaving the after-image of dear, dead George V on my startled retina.

The pipe seemed to soothe the huge fellow and, as the water bubbled in the steaming glass bowl, a look of easy contentment replaced the scowl he had worn on arrival. His good eye darted from side to side, missing nothing.

At length, he withdrew the mouthpiece of the water pipe and swivelled in my direction. A thick Newcastle accent came rather unexpectedly from his brutish Balkan form. 'I like your shoes, pet.'

'Thanks. I prefer brogues,' I replied.

'But only from Churches.'

The silly code-words exchanged, he moved sideways over the cushions and gripped my hand with his massive paw. 'All right, hinnie!' he grinned. 'You must be Lucifer Box. I've heard a lot about you.'

'Whitley Bey?' I ventured.

'None other,' he cackled. 'Didn't bring any tabs, did ya?'

'What?'

'Tabs, man! Ciggies. From England.'

'Oh – yes.' Reaching into my pocket, I retrieved my case. 'I have them made up especially. A Turkish mixture, actually—'

Whitley Bey shook his head and harrumphed. 'Nah, man. I meant Woodbines.' He caught my eye and laughed, his piratical face creasing into leathery lines. 'Aye, I know what you're thinking. All that bloody lovely tobacco out here and what's the fool want? Coffin nails! It's a long story.' He took one of my cigarettes and lit it. 'I'll have one, mind. D'you fancy a drink?'

Bey was an old contact of Delilah's and, though we'd never actually met, his reputation preceded him. Whilst maintaining a respectable public façade as a University professor, he was the secret leader of a cadre of psychoanalysts-cum-mercenaries known as the Jung Turks. Their speciality lay in imagining themselves into the minds of the enemy and then working out, through analysis, what their next move would be. If this failed, they fell back on good old-fashioned Balkan brutality. It was a potent combination and the Jung Turks were feared and respected as a result. Despite sterling work, however, keeping an eye on Soviet activities in the great melting pot of the former Constantinople, even they were soon to be absorbed into the great faceless monolith of MI6. Whitley Bey wasn't best pleased.

'I've got me own methods, you see. And they *work*,' he muttered, pouring us some wine. 'All that "Station T for Turkey" shite. Takes the fun out of it. But there you go. Anyway, listen to me bloody rabbiting on. How can I help?'

I quickly told him about the queer deaths of the elderly dignitaries, Hooplah's accident and Kingdom Kum's threats on the train.

'If the bugger's in Istanbul,' said Whitley Bey in a low voice, 'we'll find him.'

I nodded. 'Good. I hoped you'd say that. Oh, there's one more thing. Hooplah said something as he was dying.'

'Oh, aye?'

'"*Le papillon noir*" – the black butterfly. Mean anything to you?'

Bey's one good eye widened, stretching the dark skin around the sovereign. 'You interest me, Mr Box,' he said at last. 'You interest me very much.'

I drank some wine. It was rich and dark. 'How so?'

'It can get pretty rough out here,' he replied, folding his trunk-like arms. 'Gypsies. Russians. Mind, there's very little actual crime here in Istanbul. We're bloody lucky. Not many muggings. Bit of burglary . . .'

'Or Bulgary.'

'But what we do have a problem with is narcotics.'

'Oh?'

'Shite floods through here,' he went on. 'It's a gateway to the West just like it's always been. Once it was spice, now it's heroin from Afghan poppies. Then there's the other stuff. More in your prescription line. Penicillin in the war . . .'

He left a pause so pregnant it was practically having contractions.

'And now . . . ?'

'We've been picking up whispers,' he said. 'Nothing much.'

'A drug?'

Whitley Bey nodded. '"Black Butterfly". It's a new one on me.'

'Mm. Me too. It's what the French call the dumps. Depression. So – what does it do? Do you know?'

Whitley shrugged. 'That's what I hope we'll find out. Tomorrow – at the Hagia Sophia. We've got a contact on the inside.'

'The inside of the mosque?'

'The inside of the organisation. We reckon the pills are made up in a part of the city called Beyoglu. It's north of the Golden Horn. Nice area – dead posh back in the day. Up past the fish market there's a wood. Used to be a park but it's all overgrown, like. Has this big entrance like a ruddy fort. Our contact has only given us a few hints but me lads and I have pieced it together and we reckon that's their base of operations.'

I sipped some more wine. 'The drug's made there or distributed from there?'

'Your guess is as good as mine, pet.' He straightened up and stretched. 'These old gadgies who died: someone slipped them the drug, is that what you're thinking?'

'It's perfectly possible. Question is, why?'

'You reckon it's this blackie lad?'

'He's obviously up to his neck in something. And he was with Hooplah when he went berserk.'

Whitley Bey broke wind explosively and unblushingly. 'What do you wanna do now?'

I downed the rest of the wine. 'Sleep,' I said. 'After all, there's nothing we can do til we meet up with this contact of yours.'

Whitley Bey stubbed out his fag and nodded to the boy waiter. Clearly payment wasn't required. 'Aye, fair dos,' he said. 'You must be knackered. I'll call for you at nine, though them buggers in the minarets'll have you up well before that.'

.9.

MURDER IN THE CATHEDRAL

I was up and out early next morning, but the famous Istanbul bazaar was already active, heavy with the delicious scents of roasting meat and spices. Picking my way through the crowd, I suddenly felt my sleeve pulled by an ancient man wearing a suffocating brown cardigan. He grinned, exposing a nest of sugar-rotted teeth, and gestured at his treasure trove of carpets. Then Whitley Bey appeared, pushing the shopkeeper violently aside and greeting me with a thump on the back that set my own teeth rattling.

'Sleep all right, sparrow-shanks?' he asked, scooping a handful of green figs from a nearby basket. The pale sun sparkled off his sovereign eye, giving him a white-gold wink.

'Not bad,' I said.

In truth, I had not slept well at all, my mind buzzing with speculations and my fitful dreams haunted by the slim, dangerous figure of Kingdom Kum. But after a cup of sweet, strong coffee, I was feeling a little better.

We found ourselves walking slowly down a narrow alley

towards the Hagia Sophia. A boy in a striped jersey wandered past, lost in thought and scouring his nostril with a crooked finger. 'You'll forgive me for asking,' I said to Whitley, 'but you don't sound like a local man.'

He laughed explosively, and shreds of fig flew from his teeth. 'Me mam, she was Turkish, like. But me dad was from South Shields. A brickie. He come out here looking for adventure. Didn't find much, just more bricklaying. Mosques instead of churches. But he also found me mam and he married her. Then we all moved back to England till I was fifteeen. That's how comes I speak like this and why I miss cheap fags. Woodbines, man. Nowt like 'em.'

A big mongrel dog, hyena-striped with too much inter-breeding, tottered past. Its tongue lolled, improbably pink.

'I suppose you've found all the adventure your father lacked?' I said.

'Oh, hell aye. Never a dull moment,' cackled the big man.

'And this Black Butterfly contact of yours? You've met them before?'

But Whitley's contact, it seemed, was something of an enigma. Whispers about *le papillon noir* had reached the Jung Turks and they'd begun some discreet snooping. Shortly afterwards, hastily scribbled notes had been sent to Whitley's HQ at the University, promising details and the names of those involved in the drug's manufacture. The meeting in the silvery domed Byzantine wonder was to be the first physical contact between the two parties.

And now the Hagia Sophia, at various times both mosque and church, loomed before us, its spindly minarets rising like rockets into the clear blue sky. We merged with the crowd of tourists and crossed through the arched entrance. The contrast from dusty heat to chilly shadow was like stepping underwater. Sunlight pierced the wonderfully sepulchral gloom, as though dappling a reef.

High up, studding the ebony-hued balconies of the upper levels, were great Islamic roundels, chased in black and gilt, declaring the names of Allah, the Prophet and the Caliphs of old times. Huge chandeliers, like swinging incense burners, were suspended from the ceiling, and mosaic Christs gazed down blankly from the crumbling walls.

We slipped into the shadow of a fat column. 'This contact then,' I said. 'What does he look like?'

'He'll make himself known,' intoned Whitley.

'But you must have some idea.'

The big man tapped the side of his nose. I rolled my eyes, weary of this obfuscation. Whitley chuckled. 'Listen, pet. This is the East.'

'So?'

'So, when push comes to shove, things aren't so different to how they used to be in the old days – when the Turks were having their turbans nailed to their heads by bloody Draclia.'

'*Dracula*,' I corrected.

'Aye, whatever,' scowled Whitley Bey. 'The point is, you have to play by my rules or you'll get yourself in trouble, d'you understand? Once – and only once – I've let me guard down and . . .' He tapped his golden eye.

I leaned back against the pillar and said stiffly: 'What happened?'

'A gypsy took my eye with a boat-hook. Mind, I had it coming.'

'You did?'

'Aye. I was having it away with his daughters, like. Twins, man. Bloody lovely,' he laughed. 'He was well within his rights.'

I glanced over his huge shoulder as a knot of tourists began to ascend the stone stairway to the building's next level. Vulgarly dressed Germans. A lone blond boy in a red jumper with his back to me. Americans with shopping bags and cameras. Was our contact among them?

'They offered me a glass 'un,' said Whitley, tapping the coin that was screwed into his socket. 'But I says I'd rather show off me patriotic colours, like. Me dad used to have this sovereign on his watch-chain, so . . .'

'And what happened to the gypsy?'

'Too early to tell,' said Whitley in a low, dangerous voice. 'I'll think of something. One day.' His good eye swivelled round as he checked his wristwatch. 'They're late. Seen any likely candidates?'

I shook my head. 'I'll go up a level. Have a look around.'

There were too many of the broad stone steps, and I was panting by the time I reached the next floor. I crossed through the cool shadows to an ornate black balcony and looked down. Behind me, tourists began to cluster, laughing and daring each other to peek over the side.

Far below, footsteps echoed hollowly off the marble. Whitley Bey was where I'd left him, leaning casually against a pillar, and smoking. Suddenly a woman – tall, blonde and wearing a belted mackintosh – detached herself from a corner and crossed the floor.

Her heels beat a tattoo on the cold marble.

Clack, clack, clack . . .

Was she the contact?

Clack, clack, clack . . .

She was heading towards Whitley Bey. I leaned over a little too far and felt a sudden vertigo, the chamber below seeming to leap up at me. In the same instant, I noticed another figure behind a pillar, whippet thin in a charcoal suit and sunglasses. His dead straight fringe seemed to cleave his smooth face in two. Kum again!

My pulse quickened. The boy flattened himself against the stonework and pulled a pistol from his jacket. The muscles in his neck stood out like whipcord. He took aim at the woman. I opened my mouth to cry out –

– there was a soft *phut*, a gory hole appeared in the woman's forehead and she collapsed to the floor.

Appalled, I began to turn away from the balcony, only to feel a heavy shove in the small of my back. My stomach connected with the rail and suddenly I was falling through space.

Christ Almighty, or someone very like Him, zipped past my boggling gaze as I scrabbled at empty air, senses reeling, my blood turning to ice. Desperately, I managed to claw hold of something wooden, embracing it like a long-lost lover. My vision swam. Mosaic archangels with great dark, tragic, Byzantine eyes and crumbling Cyrillic texts – all span round and round. I struggled to catch my breath, then realised with a start that I was hanging onto one of the great wooden roundels next to the balcony. Now, with my nose pressed flat against the peeling woodwork, the Islamic script appeared huge in its faded gilt glory.

Attempting to get a better purchase, I stiffened as a stream of plaster trickled from the wooden frame.

'Help me!' I yelled. 'Help me, for God's sake!'

I threw a panicked glance towards the balcony. Horrified tourists looked on helplessly. I could just see the thin blond hair of the little boy in the red jumper.

'*Help me!*' I gasped, every muscle in my old limbs begging for release.

A chorus of screaming erupted from below as the masses looked up and spotted yours truly hanging there. I was desperate not to look down. I hugged the black shield, knuckles whitening, sweat flowing freely over my brow and down my back. Then I tried to shift my feet again, sending another rivulet of ancient plaster spilling over the toes of my shoes. Gasping with effort, I pressed myself even harder against the roundel and managed to haul myself up a fraction, giving me the chance to move my foot and get a tiny bit closer to the balcony.

I threw a quick look down. The floor seemed to do a giddy dance and nausea gripped me again.

Suddenly, without warning, a whole chunk of the wall gave way beneath my foot and smashed to the floor. My audience shrieked. With absolute desperation, I dug my fingernails into the ebonised woodwork and wrapped both legs about it for good measure.

Then, amongst the impotent knot of people at the balcony,

jerking out their arms towards me and gabbling away in a riot of languages appeared – thank God! – Whitley Bey!

'Hang on, hinny!' he cried. 'Just hang on!'

With no thought for his own safety, he clambered onto the balcony rail, others gripping him by his huge legs as he attempted to reach across and grab me.

Just at that moment, there was a strange, bright popping sound, as one of the bolts fixing the shield to the pillar sheared off. It sang past my ear and there was a fresh outbreak of wailing from the tourists. Then a huge sigh as, with a protesting groan, the roundel suddenly moved beneath me, turning clockwise like a great cog on its axis. I shifted my weight and splayed my fingers, as I attempted to grab hold of Whitley's outstretched hands. His thick fingers waggled, tantalisingly distant.

The big Geordie, securely held at the waist by the rest of the crowd, was now wobbling on the lip of the balcony.

'Reach, man! Reach!'

A second bolt shattered, exploding outwards. I pressed my face hard to the wood and grimaced as the lethal nugget tore past my cheek. The shield shifted again and I with it, legs akimbo. Two more bolts spat out from the masonry, leaving my fate to the solitary fixing that remained. The black shield gave a great lurch, creaking from its housing and now hanging at a perilous ninety degrees.

'Jump!' yelled Whitley Bey. 'You'll have to jump, man! It's your only chance!'

I glanced down and wished I hadn't. The gawping faces and the patterned floor sixty feet below me see-sawed as though viewed through a distorting mirror. And there was Kingdom Kum, staring up at me, the light from the chandeliers setting fire to his expensive sunglasses.

The shield groaned. There was nothing for it. I uttered a prayer to God, Allah, and whichever other deities may have been included in the building's heritage, took one great breath into my aching lungs, and leaped towards the balcony.

My hands connected with the ironwork just as the last of the bolts gave way and the massive roundel crashed to the floor in a great cloud of dust and ruined masonry.

Brown arms scrabbled over the balcony, attempting to reach me. Hands clutched at my wrists. But I'd used up the very last of my strength leaping from the shield. In spite of everything, I felt myself begin to slide from their grasp.

.10.
FINDERS, WEEPERS

Then, salvation! Whitley Bey's huge hairy hands reached down, grasped me by the shoulders and hauled me up to safety. He lowered me gently onto the balcony and deep shadow covered me. I gasped and panted, the air burning in my lungs.

'What the hell happened?' demanded Whitley.

I shook my head, scarcely able to speak.

The crowd of tourists swarmed over me like flies, questioning, cajoling, rebuking. Hands moved everywhere, checking that I was unharmed. I pushed away an elderly woman in a shawl. 'Thank you, madam,' I managed. 'I am . . . perfectly well.'

Pulling myself up, I leaned over the balcony and looked straight down. At the back of the crowd, clearly having waited to see the outcome of my fate, Kum was now beating a hasty retreat. He flashed a smile up at me, smoothed his tight trousers over his arse, and disappeared through the arched entrance.

'Him!' I croaked. 'After him!'

I grabbed Whitley by the arm and staggered towards the stairs, the stone stained red and green by the massive windows. I pushed aside some Americans, too concerned with the chase to register their protestations.

In the main chamber of the Hagia Sophia, amidst a sea of haversacks and cameras, tourists and attendants streamed over the ruined shield and the dead body of the woman in the mackintosh. Attempts were already being made to close the place. I heard the distant wail of a police siren. Whitley and I raced outside.

The sunlight was like a smack in the chops after the crypt-like gloom of the interior. The crowd outside seemed vast, jabbering, deranged, and I felt a fresh wave of nausea and disorientation. Whitley craned his neck to see over the mêlée and I struggled to follow his example, scouring the crowd for any sign of the assassin. I winced as something flashed in my line of vision. Those damned sunglasses again! I rose up on tip-toe just in time to see Kingdom Kum dive into a taxi that roared off in a cloud of mustard-coloured dust.

Playing cat and mouse again, I hailed another. It screeched to a halt before us and we collapsed gratefully into the back seats. The vehicle stank of hot plastic. I issued garbled instructions to follow the cab in front and then sank back, utterly spent.

We careered through the dust-choked streets. I wound down the window, blurred impressions slaloming past my exhausted eyes. Smoke, steam, coffee, voices. Plaster walls crumbling like white scabs. Dusty beggars clustered in corners as though they were patches of mould. A green pharmacy crescent, gently rusting. A tiny orange kitten abandoned on a square of cardboard. But no sign of Kingdom Kum. At last, exhausted and defeated, I instructed the driver to return us to my hotel.

But no sign of Kingdom Kum. At last, exhausted and defeated, I sank back into my seat. 'Brilliant! Our only contact murdered before our eyes.'

Wearily, I instructed the driver to return us to my hotel. Whitley picked at his teeth. 'The Black Butterfly people must've cottoned on to her. Sent the lad to knock her off before she could spill the beans. What now?'

I sighed, narrowing my eyes. They were gritty with dust. 'Well, they know we're onto them. They might well be preparing to up sticks.'

Whitley nodded, running a finger under his tight collar. Sweat ran down his leathery forehead. He lit one of his treasured Woodbines and coughed wheezily. 'My thoughts exactly, pet lamb. I reckon we should hit the base at Beyoglu. Hit it hard. And tonight.'

'No,' I said. 'I'm going in alone.'

Whitley Bey stared at me. 'Eh?'

'You heard me.'

'Bollocks, man,' tutted the big fellow. 'Why, you've no idea what kind of a set-up they've got in there. And we know that blackie lad's out to get you.'

I patted the reassuring bulk of the Steyr in its shoulder-holster. 'We need information,' I said. Detailed information.

And for that, stealth is the best weapon. I used to be pretty good at this lark. Give me an hour and then come in all guns blazing. Deal?'

He shrugged. 'All right, hinnie. But listen, I've got some equipment you might find useful. You get your head down and some of me lads'll pop it round later.'

'Equipment?'

'You'll see.' He shook his great head, setting his earrings jangling but then clapped me on the shoulder. 'Your funeral, sparrow-shanks. But you're the boss.'

'Yes,' I said, smiling. 'I am.'

Dusk was settling over the city like sleep, casting long purple shadows. A velvet-gentle night wind caught the call to prayer and took its siren wail across the rooftops of 'Stamboul. We drove up the Istiklal Caddesi towards the malodorous fish market. I don't think I've ever felt so done up. But I knew I had to press on – to the neglected park in the Beyoglu district of which Whitley had spoken.

The fort-like entrance was a strange, disquieting sort of place; its brown bricks flat as Biblical loaves; the ragged walls serrated like teeth. Under an archway sat an old man in a filthy smock, staring ahead with incurious brown eyes. Behind him, the tumbled walls led into the abandoned park, the trees nothing but clumps of blackness in the dying light.

Whitley and I got out of the car and I glanced up. Kestrels were wheeling in the indigo sky, keening, cheeping.

'My lads'll be here in one hour,' said Whitley softly. 'Then we come in, all right?'

'Scout's honour,' I said, then moved swiftly towards the track that led up to the entrance. Swirling dust sprang up around me like a company of ghosts. Keeping well away from the sentinel in the archway, I pressed myself close to the wall and crept round until I found a narrow, glassless window. Cautiously, I clambered up onto the stone sill and squeezed myself through, conscious of my aching muscles and the bruises I'd sustained at the Hagia Sophia. Beyond was blackness but I resisted the urge to spark up my lighter, instead taking a few moments for my eyes to adjust.

The interior of the fort was little more than rubble. There were patches of a mosaic floor and rather beautiful Islamic carvings over a few of the shattered doorways. I glanced down to see a pale yellow scorpion executing tiny, mincing steps over my shoe. I kicked it away and, keeping low, headed across the rocky debris towards the back of the structure.

Trees that twisted like unset limbs formed an arched opening to the woodland, rather like a stage set. I passed through and, almost at once, silence swamped me.

I moved on, the ground thick with pine needles, and unseen burrs whipping at my trousers. The air was heavy with the dank, mossy smell of the forest. Branches whipped at my face and every step was hard work. With no clear pathway and devilishly uneven ground, I was constantly ducking under overhanging branches and, in the blackness, barking my shins on long-fallen, moss-swaddled trunks.

Suddenly, I emerged into a clearing. Starkly lit by arc lamps, there stood a complex of steel buildings, enclosed on all sides by high wire mesh. The glass that made up almost half the structure gave the place a cool, restrained glamour. There were huge tanks, like gasometers, dotted around the perimeter, each labelled with a skull and crossbones. As I watched, automatic steel doors shushed open and figures in white laboratory coats glided in and out.

Creeping carefully through nettles that stood as tall as my thigh, I made my way towards the perimeter fence. Almost at once, a fat uniformed guard rounded the corner, a muscular Doberman straining on a tight lead before him. The hound gazed about, its master doing likewise until both were swallowed up in the darkness as the sweeping beam of the searchlight passed by. I looked at the hands of my Girard Perregaux watch. Fifteen minutes of my precious hour had already gone.

Time to employ Whitley Bey's equipment! I unbuckled my belt, and, using the tiny hacksaw blade concealed within, made short work of the fence. I cut three sides of a large square and then kicked at the wire until it bent right back. Seconds later, I was through. Pushing the mesh back into place, I raced to the nearest wall and flattened myself against it just in time, as the searchlight illuminated the path where I'd stood. Shuffling along, I came to a small, barred window and, cupping my hands around my eyes, strained to peer within. The room beyond was in darkness, but I began to make out sheeted shapes. Just chairs and tables. I moved on until, around the next corner, I found what I was looking for. A large truck was parked outside, its rear end open and a forklift busily unloading large pallets.

A man with a clipboard was supervising. As well as the regulation lab coat, he was sporting a kind of gas-mask, presumably as defence against whatever toxic substance was contained in the tanks. In the stark striplighting from the loading bay beyond, the eye-holes were a queasy green colour and the mask itself semi-transparent. Still, I thought grimly, it would suit my purpose.

Now all I had to do was to attract the chap's attention. I rapidly considered my options – everything from hooting like an owl to rolling coins towards him – when the decision was taken out of my hands. The forklift suddenly gave an unhealthy sort of rattle, stalled and rolled backwards, upsetting the pallet that was balanced on the twin prongs and scattering what looked like aspirin pills all over the dusty yard.

Pills! Was this 'Black Butterfly'?

The gas-masked supervisor immediately threw up his hands in horror. He wrenched open the forklift's cabin door and berated the driver in a stream of incomprehensible oaths. The driver, fat and also masked, wearing a too-tight T-shirt, shrugged and muttered and swore back, clearly believing the accident to be no fault of his.

The supervisor sighed heavily, stepped back into the shadows to make a note on his clipboard and then made a high, surprised gurgling sound as my arm snaked round his neck and squeezed him into unconsciousness. In moments, I reappeared, holding the clipboard and adjusting the mask over my white hair. I made a rude gesture to the forklift driver, and then I was through the door, eager to put as much distance between myself and the harsh light of the exterior.

I found myself in a warm, inevitably white corridor. A series of rectangular windows was inset in the wall and appeared to look down onto rooms below, like the viewing galleries of an operating theatre. The corridor terminated in a set of stairs.

I moved towards the first of the windows, the gas-mask tasting foul and rubbery, but then a low beeping sound close by warned me that another of the steel doors was about to open. I rapidly pressed myself into a recessed alcove in which stood some hideous specimen of modern sculpture, all wire and bronze. Two white-coated men strode past, their steps soft and noiseless in white moccasins.

I waited a moment, then crossed back to the window, ripping off the gas-mask so I could see more clearly. The room below was bathed in a purplish light, banks of machinery in a wide crescent taking up most of the space, along with some kind of viewing screen. On it was projected a huge map of the world, various cities ringed in yellow. In the curious light, everything showed up with weird vividness, as though the whole room were submerged in a lagoon.

Puzzling over what this could mean, I stole further along the corridor. Soon I reached another window. I kept close to the wall, all too aware of the pearly light bleeding up from below, edged to the side and risked a peek down.

Stretched out on a padded table lay a male form, naked save for his white underwear. His hip-bones showed over the waistband, prominent as razor-shells. The arms and legs were long and brown, the soles of the feet much paler.

A white-coated figure in a surgical mask hovered at the

head-end of the table, then suddenly stepped back, like a painter from a canvas, as though admiring his handiwork.

And revealed, lying there, eyes closed and hair plastered to his sweat-soaked forehead like a raven's wing, was Kingdom Kum.

.11.
DÉTENTE

The boy resembled the Descended Christ. A Regnault, perhaps, the crisp white underwear in place of a loincloth.

Tick-tock, baby. Tick-tock.

My mind buzzed. What the hell was going on?

The masked figure returned to Kum's prone form. He held something in his hand. Some instrument of torture, I imagined, but the angle of the plate glass and the glare of the huge surgical lamps conspired to obscure it from my view.

I gazed down at the youth, noticing the tiny handful of wiry hairs scattered over the hard, flat pads of his chest muscles. In my mind, conflicting thoughts tumbled over one another. He'd been in at the death of Vyvyan Hooplah. Then, on the train, he'd tried unsuccessfully to warn me off. Finally, he'd shot dead Whitley's contact in the Hagia Sophia. So what had he done to displease his masters? Why was he lying there, presumably about to suffer some unspeakable agony?

The lad lay completely still, leather straps binding him tightly to the operating table. Was he already unconscious, I wondered, or merely sleeping?

The answer came out of the blue as his heavy-lidded eyes fluttered open. In a vain attempt to secure anonymity, I fumbled for my gas-mask. Too late. Kingdom Kum's almond eyes focused on me, and a befuddled frown of recognition passed across his face.

Now what?

I swore softly to myself as I saw him nodding upwards in my direction. His torturer span round, and he too became aware of my silvery head bobbing at the window.

Rooted to the spot, I watched as the white-coated man strode across to a console on the far side of the room. Leaning over, he flicked a small red switch. In the corridor, a Tannoy system crackled into life.

'Kemal?' came the technician's voice, his heavy accent distorted further by the microphone. 'Where the hell have you been? Stop gawping and get yourself down here, will you? This one is tough.'

I weighed up my options. If I made a run for it, the torturer would become suspicious and no doubt alert others. On the other hand, I'd come seeking information. I would see what I could discover! So, fastening the straps on the gas-mask and hoping that, with my face obscured, I could somehow pass for the missing Kemal, I made my way down the stairs.

By the time I entered the operating theatre, the white-coated torturer had returned to the captive Kingdom Kum. 'Now,' he hissed at the semi-naked youth, 'you will start talking. You will die, of course. How quickly and how painlessly, my friend, is entirely your decision.'

Kingdom Kum remained silent.

The torturer chuckled menacingly. 'So you are the tough guy, yes? Like in the John Wayne pictures, yes? Well, we shall see how long that lasts.'

White-coat paused and glanced over at me. 'What's the matter with you today, Kemal? Must I do everything myself? Oh, and take your gas-mask off, you coward. There's nothing dangerous in here.' He resumed his appraisal of Kingdom Kum. 'Well, apart from me, that is.'

Silently, I made my way over, and stood just behind the torturer's right shoulder.

Kum turned his head towards me and stared intently into my face. Then slowly, insolently, he spoke to White-coat. 'I'm telling you nothing, baby. But your friend here – if he asks nicely, can find out everything I know about Black Butterfly.'

What strange game was this? Was he bargaining for his life?

Then things happened very quickly. Turning to face me properly for the first time, a look of confusion crossed the torturer's face.

'Hey,' he accused. 'You're not—'

I lashed out with my fist, catching the fellow under the chin. He was flung against the wall and crumpled into a white heap.

He reached into his coat for a gun but I was instantly on top of him, pummelling him into unconsciousness with rapid blows from my balled fists.

From the operating table came a soft chuckle. 'Man,' said Kingdom Kum, 'you've still got it.'

'All right, my friend,' I snapped. 'Now would you mind telling me what the hell is going on?'

'I said you had to ask nicely, Mr Box,' grinned the youth.

I aimed the Steyr at his face. 'This is as nice as I'm feeling right now,' I hissed. 'Talk.'

Kum shook his head. 'No time. We have to get out of here fast.'

I snorted with derision. 'So now you're expecting me to help you *escape*?'

'Come on, baby. You saw the mess I was in. You honestly think I'd be strapped to this thing if I was working for these goons? Believe me, we have to leave, and we can help each other do it.'

Every instinct within me protested and yet, moments later, I had released Kingdom Kum's shackles. Old Boxy getting soft, you might think, eh? Well, not so fast. I wasn't taking any chances. Now, I may be a fool for a pretty face, but this was not the time to let my guard down.

'Warily, I released Kingdom Kum's shackles and then watched as he struggled into his torturer's clothes. Soon the two of us were walking swiftly from the operating theatre, gas-masks firmly in place, the Steyr in the small of the youth's back.

In the corridor, we passed no one apart from a sweating technician rushing in the opposite direction – presumably the tardy Kemal. I intended to get the two of us out of there pronto, and meet up with Whitley Bey and his men in the forest. My 'hostage', however, had other ideas. He pulled up abruptly outside a white door marked *No Entry*.

'We need to go in here,' he told me.

'That way's forbidden,' I said.

Kingdom Kum grinned. 'Like all the best things.'

My suspicions were raised instantly. '*Why* do we need to go in there?'

The youth pushed his unruly fringe from his eyes. 'I know you have no reason to trust me, baby—'

'None at all, Mr Kum. None at all.'

He regarded me with his inky eyes. 'Look, there's something I need to take from here. You have three options. Either you go now and let me get it on my own. Or you come with me and we help each other get out of here alive.'

'That's only two.'

'The third option is you shoot me. 'Cos I'm not leaving without it.' His flippancy had deserted him and there was a glint of the steel I'd witnessed on the train.

'All right,' I sighed. 'We'll do it your way, but cross me and I'll kill you. *Baby*.'

The boy giggled and pressed his hand to his throat. 'Thanks, toots. You're a doll.'

Stealthily, he pushed open the door, and we found ourselves in a darkened, rather airless room. To our left, the wall was composed entirely of narrow drawers such as might contain seed specimens.

'They're moving out,' Kum told me enigmatically. 'The work here is pretty much done.'

'What work?' I asked quietly.

But the boy didn't answer, just slipped noiselessly into the shadows and began rooting through the drawers. Each one whispered open to his touch. After the harsh white light of the corridor, my senses took a while to adjust. The room wasn't quite as empty as it had first appeared but was in a pretty chaotic state. Scattered across wooden surfaces was a variety of scientific instruments: microscope slides, Petri dishes, syringes and all manner of other stuff I couldn't identify.

Kingdom Kum was still busy at the bank of white drawers. I was making my way over towards the instruments when I became aware of a strange sound: a gentle drumming. A fluttering, beating noise, barely perceptible at first, but increasing in volume as I neared the far wall. Then I realised that the wall behind the laboratory work benches was actually thick, velvety drapes.

Curious, I dragged them back and let out a long, slow breath. Revealed was a vast butterfly enclosure, a lepidopterium, I suppose: its thousands of black inhabitants colliding against one another in that stuffy, crowded environment. Particles of dust hung like pollen in the air.

I peered through the clear glass. They were large creatures, and their fat, hairy bodies made my skin crawl.

'Pretty, huh?' came the murmur of Kingdom Kum from across the other side of the lab.

'*Les papillons noirs*?'

'Properly speaking, hun, *papilio obscurus*,' he whispered. 'But the high-school lecture can wait. If you're done there, I've got what I need.' He held up a slim glass tube before my face, and rattled the contents.

'And what's that?'

Kingdom Kum laughed his flutey laugh and waggled a finger at me. 'Naughty, baby. No questions. Not now.'

Seconds later, we were back in the corridor. I gestured with the gun towards the exit door. Then the cotton wool silence was ripped apart by the scream of a klaxon.

I glanced at my watch. The hour was more than up. Whitley Bey's men had arrived! Distantly, I heard the thrum-thrum of machine-gun fire.

There was a sudden clatter of feet and two white-coated men came haring down the corridor. They boggled at us and then one reached for his pistol. I swung round and shot him through the heart. As he slumped to the tiled floor, I brought my gas-mask smartly round and smashed the other one across the face. He was instantly out cold.

Then the two of us raced through the doors.

Outside, the air was alive with smoky scents.

I tore off the lab coat. My black suit would provide an infinitely more useful camouflage in the forest. Kingdom Kum kept his on, shivering a little in his hastily thrown-on ensemble.

I found the hole in the fence that I'd cut on my way in, and once again bashed it down. We scuttled through: first the boy and then myself. Keeping low, we put on some speed and made for the safety of the forest.

After five minutes of running, I was exhausted.

'Hang on,' I gasped. 'Give me a moment.'

Kingdom Kum nodded and I sank back against the gnarled bark of a tree, slowing my breathing. The sweeping arc of light from the clinic silhouetted the slender trees, turning them into prison bars. I reached into my trousers and pulled out another of Whitley Bey's little miracles – a sachet of rehydration fluid, one of several sewn into the lining below my belt.

I drank it gratefully and then turned to offer one to my companion.

Oh, how inevitable! I was alone in the forest. Kingdom Kum had charmed me, duped me, and had now made his escape.

Gunfire crackled from the distant clinic, and the blare of a klaxon made me wince. I heard shouting coming from behind me.

I decided my best course of action would be to get out of the vicinity as rapidly as my aged legs would carry me. Somewhat revitalised by the rehydration sachet, I fell into a slow jog. However, I had gone only a few hundred yards when a hulking silhouette barred the path before me. I pulled up and ducked behind the nearest tree, hoping that I'd been in time to avoid detection.

'Alright, petal,' said the shape. 'Eeh, I can't leave you alone for five minutes, can I?'

It was Whitley Bey.

And, clamped in the crook of his immense forearm, gasping for air, struggled the elusive Kingdom Kum.

I gave a huge sigh of relief – then suddenly the forest lit up like day. There was a terrific explosion and the three of us were hurled to the ground.

.12.
THE KEYS TO THE KINGDOM

Rain was tipping down outside the long window but, in the dimness of the University, a three-barred electric fire glowed cheerfully.

Just as promised, Whitley Bey had given me my hour's grace and then he and his men had hit the enemy headquarters with everything they had. Unfortunately, it seemed the place was booby-trapped and so, seconds after the Jung Turks had shot their way inside, the building had gone up in flames. In the chaos, the few white-coated figures who had survived the attack had managed to escape, leaving behind little evidence of their activities. At least, though, we had Kingdom Kum.

He was huddled in a thick blanket before the fire, staring into space.

Whitley Bey sat bass-ackwards in a chair, paring his nails with a brutal-looking knife and shooting resentful glares at the newcomer. I stretched out my aching legs and lit a cigarette, letting the strains of the last few hours fall away. My ears still rang from the explosion.

I proffered my fag case to Kingdom Kum. He grabbed one and popped it between his lips. I leaned across with my lighter and he inhaled hungrily, then glanced quickly back and forth between Whitley and myself. There was something of the trapped beast about him – feral, suspicious, dangerous.

I cleared my throat and said: 'Now, isn't this nice? I believe I invited you to do some talking back there, Mr Kum. Why don't you start?'

The boy pulled a shred of tobacco from between his teeth and glanced down at his long, bare feet. 'Damn. I had some nice shoes back there in the clinic. Cost a mint.' He shivered. 'I was particularly fond of those shoes. Burned up now, I guess?'

I nodded. 'I said, *talk*.'

'Wasn't I *just* talking?'

'Don't get smart. Who exactly are you working for?'

The boy shrugged. 'I don't have time for this, toots. You gotta let me go.'

Whitley Bey made a low, growling sound. 'Shall I smack him about a bit? Sweat the truth out of him?'

'No,' I said flatly. 'Not yet, anyway.' I raised my eyebrows at the youth. The threat was implicit.

He sighed, then took a long drag on the cigarette. 'Hey, you think I could sue those guys? Get some replacements? They were damned fine shoes—'

Whitley Bey rose from his chair like a Titan from the waves, hand balling into a fist. 'Stop buggering us about, you little ponce!'

I stilled him with a gesture. He sank back into his chair, rumbling.

Kingdom Kum smiled. 'I'm what they call a rare bird, baby. Momma from Osaka, Daddy from Jamaica. There weren't many like us at home. Daddy's boss coined a name for me and my sister. *Japanegroes*.'

'How did you feel about that?'

'I didn't care for it. Or him.'

I searched my memory. 'This was Mr . . . *Hyogo*?'

The boy laughed his fluting laugh. 'You remembered, baby! *Très* sweet.'

'Aha,' I said. 'So much for your father's boss. Who's yours?'

Kingdom Kum just smiled, letting smoke pour from his nostrils like a patient dragon. Whitley sighed heavily and turned to me, metal eye glinting. 'We'll get nowt out of this one, Mr Box. You should've left him in there.'

The boy sucked on the cigarette again and his eyes closed in a long, exhausted blink. 'I'm most grateful you didn't.' He hugged the blanket closer to his skinny frame and let ash tumble down it. 'Listen, baby. You gotta trust me.'

Whitley laughed explosively. 'Now I've heard everything.' He leaned towards the boy and I could smell the sweat from his bear-like frame. 'Answer Mr Box's question. Who the hell are you working for? *Who?*'

'Don't you mean "for whom are you working"?'

Before I could stop him, Whitley had shot from his chair and smacked the youth across the face. 'You cheeky get!' he spat. 'I'll bloody crown you!'

Kingdom Kum's long fingers flashed to his cheek and his dark eyes narrowed with malice. 'We shouldn't be sitting here playing games.'

'I couldn't agree more,' I murmured. 'Back on the train, you warned me off—'

'Maybe I just like your face.'

'—and then you killed our contact in the Hagia Sophia . . .'

Kingdom Kum began giggling in his sing-song way and pressed a long slender hand to his throat. 'Man, you are in the *dark*. You have no idea!'

'All right, then,' I bristled. 'Enlighten us.'

'Can I get some clothes, baby?'

'I don't think so, *baby*.'

He shrugged the blanket closer. 'I know this sounds crazy but you gotta let me go. Certain . . . persons ain't gonna be too happy if you don't.'

I smoothed down my waistcoat. 'Is that another threat?'

'Uh-huh.'

I shook my head in disbelief. 'You're a cool one and no mistake. But you seem to forget who's in charge here.'

He looked down so that all I could see was a flash of his white teeth through the black tumble of his hair. 'You've put your finger right on it,' he whispered.

Whitley Bey's chair squeaked as he rose again, fist raised.

I nodded towards the door. 'All right, Whitley. I'll take it from here.'

'You sure? Go on, let us do him over a bit. Never fails, man. 'Specially with a smart little shite-hawk like this.'

'No,' I rapped. 'I'll see you later.'

Reluctantly, the big man stomped from the office, taking time to throw one last snarl towards the boy.

Kingdom Kum stretched out his long legs and regarded his

bare feet as though still mourning the loss of his shoes. Then he looked up, head on one side, like a nervous bird. 'Hey, handsome. Did I say thanks?'

'Thanks?'

'For rescuing me.'

'As a matter of fact, you didn't. In fact, you behaved rather rudely. Trying to run off like that.'

He shook his head, leaned over and slipped a single digit through my fingers and into my palm, moving it around in a neat circle. 'You wanna let me make it up to you?'

I pulled my hand away, heart pounding and all too conscious of the heat and the scent of the boy. I was still smarting from Miss Beveridge and the humiliation of the cemetery.

Suddenly, I heard raised voices in the outer office. Whitley Bey sounded angry. I frowned.

Kingdom Kum scraped back the hair from his face. 'You wanted some answers, yes?'

I nodded.

'Then you're in luck, baby,' he said, stubbing out his fag.

The door opened to reveal a rain-soaked figure. He shook out his umbrella and waved a silly little wave. 'Fear not! Only me,' said Allan Playfair.

My face fell. 'What are you doing here?'

Playfair crossed to the fire and warmed his hands. 'I'm coming to the end, old love, of a very long game.'

.13.
REALPOLITIK

Another hotel room. A long way from Istanbul. Beyond the balcony, the lights of Kingston, Jamaica, sparkled like cut-glass.

Allan Playfair tossed his straw hat onto the bed and plonked himself next to me. His cane-backed chair creaked. A warm breeze blew across us, a gentle caress after the heat of the day. 'Well, old love. This is the life, eh?'

I said nothing. I'd spent the long journey to Kingston quietly frustrated. There'd been no explanations, scarcely a chance to say farewell to a baffled-looking Whitley Bey and, after a whispered conference between Playfair and Kingdom Kum, I'd been bundled into a taxi to the airport. Playfair had promised to tell me everything on our arrival. Well, I was all ears.

He tapped his pipe on the iron balustrade and grinned to himself. 'If this is the sort of lark our agents get up to, I might have to trade in that desk job, what? Get myself a Beretta, a pretty girl and an expense account.'

I leaned back in my chair and closed my eyes. 'Would it be too much to ask, *old love*, what the bloody hell's going on?'

He stuffed tobacco into his pipe, spent a moment lighting it and the air was soon suffused with its sweet cherry-smell. 'You really mustn't be cross,' he said, glancing over. 'It wasn't meant to be like this at all. But your trouble is, you're so damned good.'

'Good?' I snorted. 'I've been blundering around like a blasted mole, when all along my own people, so it seems, have known about the whole thing.'

Playfair shook his head. '*Au contraire*. You got a lead via the strange behaviour of Sir Vyvyan Hooplah. That led you to Istanbul and finally to the clinic where you were good enough to save the life of Mr Kum. Very nicely done.' He looked at me over his pipe and pulled a face. 'Trouble is, you very nearly blew many months of careful planning and—'

I sat up, stiff with anger. 'I was promised answers.'

'Fire away, old love.'

I tried to marshal my thoughts. 'Hooplah's death. It wasn't the first of its kind.'

Playfair pointed the stem of his pipe at me. 'Spot on.'

'Sir Douglas Gobetween, Baroness Watchbell and that French priest,' I said. 'All of them died in bizarre, reckless accidents.'

Playfair chuckled. 'No flies on you, old love. But did you discover the connection?'

I shrugged. '"Black Butterfly"?'

'Top marks.'

I hunched forward. 'So, this new drug—'

'Well, that's just the thing, old love,' Playfair corrected me. 'It's not *new* at all.'

'I don't follow.'

Playfair got up and poured us both a cool gin. 'Turns out it was something we were working on years ago. The forces of light, that is. Back at the turn of the century, in fact.' He grinned. 'Your heyday.'

I took the glass with ill grace.

'It's distilled from the wings of the *papilio obscurus*,' he continued. 'Found only in the Balkans. Butterflies have a sort of dust on their scales. I remember it from when I was a boy. If you brush it off, the poor things die. Dear me, what blood-thirsty devils we were then. I used to get a magnifying glass and—'

'Yes, yes!' I snapped. 'This dust . . . ?'

Playfair pulled his pipe from his mouth. 'It acts like a psychotropic drug. Induces temporary euphoria and an incredible increase in the metabolic rate. Back in the day, the thinking was it might be very useful on the battlefield. Indestructible soldiers and so forth, you see?'

I turned weary eyes towards him. 'There's a *but* coming, isn't there? I can always sense a *but*.'

'The stuff was lethal,' said Playfair. 'Drove its subjects off their heads. Induced strokes. Heart failure. All round, a disaster. So the project was abandoned.'

I rubbed my bristly chin. 'And the project's team members . . . ?'

'Right again. Gobetween as Defence Secretary sanctioned the experiments. Baroness Watchbell—'

'Pharmacist.'

'Yes. She and Père Meddler headed the scientific team. And Vyvyan Hooplah as Head of the Board of Health was obviously keen to keep a weather eye on their progress.'

I looked out over the balcony towards the crashing sea. 'So this is – what? – some kind of revenge scheme? Someone's using a new form of the drug to kill off the people originally responsible for it?'

Playfair swirled the ice around his glass and took a small sip. 'That's what we reckon. Outstanding questions being *who* and *why*.'

'What about Christopher Miracle?'

'Who?'

I sighed. 'Old friend of mine. I told you about him. Drove his car into the sea off Cape Town.'

'Oh, yes. I remember.'

'It's the same pattern.'

'Is it?' Playfair shrugged. 'Just a suicide, surely?'

I chewed a fingernail. 'He was nothing to do with the original drug trial?'

'Never heard of him, old love. Must just be coincidence. Top-up?'

I shook my head impatiently. 'I have another outstanding question for you. Who the hell is Kingdom Kum?'

'Can't you guess?' Playfair asked softly. 'Really, one can't make a move without the Yanks these days.'

'CIA?' I offered.

Playfair jabbed his pipe again and nodded. 'He's quite a live wire, isn't he? Damned good field agent. He pieced together the whole thing. That's why he was in London. He knew the "Black Butterfly" people were after Hooplah. Traced him to the *Blood Orange* but someone had already slipped the old fellow the pill. He got there too late . . . Well, you know the rest.'

'But the girl in the Hagia Sophia,' I protested. 'He killed *her*!'

'Before *she* could murder that interesting Turkish gorilla you'd befriended, old love. There was no *contact* out to betray "Black Butterfly". They knew that the Jung Turks were sniffing round, so they fed them just enough titbits to intrigue the silly fools and then arranged to meet Whitley Bey and put him out of the way.'

I gazed at him coolly.

'After that,' said Playfair, 'Mr Kum tried to infiltrate their headquarters but was captured. Happily, you turned up to save the day, so all was not lost—'

'Listen,' I cut in. 'In case you've forgotten, your bloody merger doesn't take effect for another month! I'm still "Joshua Reynolds". You should have told me about this narcotics business. We could've shared information.'

Playfair frowned and his expression hardened just a mite. 'Look, old love. You know how it is. I don't wish to be unkind but you're yesterday's man. You should be thinking about fishing flies, not tearing around the Balkans like a stripling. Damn it, Box, it's undignified. I have to deal with the here and now. *Realpolitik*, old love. *Realpolitik*.'

'So why are we here – in Jamaica?'

'The last link in the chain,' said Playfair, setting down his gin. 'The remaining target in this curious revenge. Lord Battenburg.'

'Battenburg? Why the hell?'

'He discovered the *papilio obscurus* butterfly itself on some Boy's Own adventure of his out in the wilds. Then happened upon its extraordinary properties once back in his laboratory. Anyway, he's coming out here the day after tomorrow to open the World Government Summit.' Playfair drained his glass. 'Lord Battenburg is the last target. Kingdom Kum found out that much before he was captured. That, and the fact that they're planning to get him here, in Jamaica.'

I let this rather startling intelligence sink in. 'So why are we sitting here?' 'Why aren't you doing something, Playfair?'

'I *am* doing something,' he said tartly. 'Everything's in hand. I've taken personal charge of Lord Battenburg's security. We've got people tasting everything he eats and drinks.'

I shook my head in disbelief. 'He must cancel the summit meeting! It's far too dangerous.'

'No, no, no,' soothed Playfair. 'We need to learn the lesson of History, old love. You, of all people, should appreciate that. We need to let the conspiracy mature. Like they did with the Gunpowder plotters. You remember?'

'Incredible as it may seem, I wasn't actually around in the seventeenth century.'

Playfair chuckled. 'Oh, we will miss you, old love. You're a *card* and no mistake. But don't you see? We still have no idea who's behind the whole ruddy scheme. We have to let their plans take their course so we can nip in and grab the whole gang.'

I shook my head and knocked back the rest of my gin. Playfair's eyebrows rose.

'It's madness,' I said. 'And it doesn't add up. There's . . . there's something wrong.'

'What, exactly?'

'It just feels . . .' I shrugged helplessly.

'Security is watertight,' said Playfair.

'*Really?*'

'Abso-bloomin'-lutely,' he smiled, steepling his fingers. 'Battenburg has handpicked them himself. Boys in whom he has the utmost confidence.'

'And where do I fit in?'

'Well,' drawled Playfair, 'I thought you'd like to be in on the kill, as it were. Nice big coup for the Service. Handing over the baton and all that.'

I rose to my feet, a little drunk. 'No, thanks.'

'No?'

'You'll forgive me, I'm sure. But I think I've seen quite enough.'

I grabbed my jacket and stalked from the room.

In Jamaica they call the wind that blows in from the centre of the island, the Undertaker's Wind. It stirred my snowy hair and made me shiver despite the balminess of the violet evening. I stood in the hotel lobby, the door ajar.

I was absolutely bloody furious. I'd been patronised, misled and ignored.

And what of Kingdom Kum? Was it genuine respect that had made him try to warn me off, back on the train? I'd saved his life in the clinic, but had his thanks been sincere? Or was he touched the way a dog-owner is when his old pooch unexpectedly manages a trick its arthritic limbs have long ago prevented? But then I remembered his finger stroking my palm and the wonderful heat of him in that tiny, dark room . . .

I walked to the front desk and asked for Kingdom's room. A sweating concierge in a heavy uniform told me that Mr Kum was on the second floor in Room 209.

I could go up and see him. There had been something there, beneath the boy's bravado, I was sure of it. And I could do with some affection.

But I didn't go upstairs. Instead, I left the hotel and walked beneath the palms that lined the driveway. I was Lucifer Box. And I didn't *need* anyone.

The blare of a car horn snapped me from my reverie and I watched as a flotilla of limousines glided past on the main road, the flags on their bonnets fluttering. No doubt various dignitaries arriving for the World Government Summit. The cars drew up outside a huge, domed conference centre. They were busy people. In a hurry. Not yesterday's men.

I cursed my self-pity and tried to pull myself together.

Out on the promenade, the sea was indistinguishable from the night sky but the glowing lights of a ship thrilled with their own romance. I listened to the sound of the surf and then to the shuffle of my shoes on the cracked pavement. I scarcely glanced at the various restaurants and shops that lined the sea-front. Then a harsh, flapping sound made me look up.

I was in front of what looked like some kind of concert hall, cream-painted and monumental. It was flanked on both sides by flagpoles that rattled in the breeze. Long skeins of fabric had been attached to them lengthways and I squinted to make out the design on them: a fleur-de-lys. I stepped closer. Under the emblem, picked out in black on gold was the legend *The Great Scout Jamboree*.

I stopped dead, baffled. Then it dawned on me. Of course! The Jamboree! I'd only half-listened, back when I'd taken Christmas to that wretched Scout camp. Was it possible? Not Kingston-on-Thames but Kingston, *Jamaica*? Could my little boy be *here*? I felt a sudden, very pressing and slightly tipsy need to see the little mite. Now I knew I really had hit a low point. I should see a doctor.

I walked up the wide marble steps to the building's entrance and glanced at my watch. It was a little after seven. Surely there'd still be someone around who could tell me where the Jamboree was being held or even where Christmas was staying.

I approached the glass doors of the concert hall. Within, a desk lamp was the only illumination. I cupped my hand over my eyes and peered inside. As there was no sign of life, I tried the door. To my surprise, it opened and I entered a high-ceilinged lobby.

The silence was as deep as the carpet.

'Hello?'

No response. I padded towards the desk. A cigarette was burning in an ashtray, grey smoke idling towards the ceiling. I presumed its owner had stepped out for a moment. I decided to wait.

A muffled flush explained the smoker's absence and I turned towards the sound. A door opened and a slender silhouette appeared. It stopped sharply at the sight of me.

'Yes?' came a woman's voice.

'I wonder if you could help me,' I said. 'I'm enquiring about the Scout Jamboree . . .'

The figure stepped into the light. It was Melissa ffawthawte! It felt like months since that game of snooker back at the camp.

'Why, it's Mr Box, isn't it?' she said, cocking her head to one side.

'My dear Miss ffawthawte! How very nice to see you again.'

She batted her eyelashes. 'You've come all this way just for a re-match?'

Considering the tone of our last encounter, she now seemed oddly coquettish. What *was* going on?

'Ha, ha. Not quite. I'm . . . passing through. Just wondered how my son—'

'Oh, you wish to see little Christmas? How sweet.'

'Well, yes,' I said. 'Is he here?'

'Alas, you can't visit him tonight. Early to bed, early to rise . . .'

'Oh well, not to worry,' I muttered. 'Perhaps tomorrow?'

'That would be fine,' said Miss ffawthawte, making a note in the desk diary. 'Shall we say two o'clock?'

'Smashing. So . . . do tell. What have the kiddie-winkies been getting up to? Got them well trained, have you?'

'Oh, yes!' she enthused, tossing back the coils of her silky brown hair. 'Very well trained. And soon there'll be a public demonstration of this. A very public demonstration.'

'Capital! Well, good night, then. Thank you for all your help. I do hope—'

The words died on my lips. In the dim light from the desk lamp, I'd suddenly noticed something. Miss ffawthawte's bosom was slightly more exposed than when I'd last seen her. Now I saw almost all of her tattoo, the merest hint of which had so thrilled me in the games room. It was a Black Butterfly.

Melissa ffawthawte narrowed her green eyes and glanced down at her breasts. 'Dear me. How careless.'

In one smooth movement, she pulled a long-barrelled pistol from her jacket. There was a soft swishing sound, I felt a sharp pain in the neck and knew nothing more.

.14.
'ARE YOU DYING COMFORTABLY?'

The globular light overhead was like an eyeball dangling from a nerve.

Heavy leather straps bound me to a table at the ankles, across the chest and over the neck. My hands were secured by tight leather cuffs. An insistent itch on my throat reminded where the tranquilliser dart had hit home.

The room around me, glass-walled, green-tinged at its bevelled edges, refused to stay still: juddering, shifting, like a ropey television picture. I winced at the intensity of the surgical lights, screwing shut my wrinkled old orbits. Then, after a few deep breaths, I tentatively looked again.

How long had I been there?

A metal door opened and soft footsteps padded close by. From my restricted vantage point, I could see only a whitish blob and then, suddenly, a face loomed startlingly over mine, the lower half concealed by a surgical mask, the hair tucked away inside a white cap. Green eyes blazed down.

'Are you quite comfortable, Mr Box?' asked Melissa ffawthawte.

'Not at all.'

'Glad to hear it. I must say, I'm impressed. You are a game old thing.'

I beamed. 'You're too kind.'

My exhausted mind was reeling from this new development. What the hell did Melissa ffawthawte have to do with the whole 'Black Butterfly' set-up?

All at once, she disappeared from sight. Unable to move, I thought at first she'd left the room but then, with a squeal of wheels, a stool was dragged over towards the table. She sat down and there was a soft sigh from the padded white seat.

'Now then,' she breathed. 'It's rather important that you tell me what you know – or think you know – about what we're doing here.'

'Is it now? How lovely.'

'And we have ways and means of extracting such information.'

I strained at my bonds and the leather creaked. 'Ah. I thought we might get around to that.'

'So why don't we save ourselves a lot of unpleasantness,' mused the girl. 'Just pucker up, Mr Box, and whisper some sweet nothings in my ear.'

'That's just what I will whisper.'

'Hm?'

'Nothing.'

She crossed her legs – rather sensational in white stockings – and gave a little snigger. 'We'll see.'

The wheels of the stool squealed again as she pulled herself closer to the table.

'I'm a specialist,' she said quietly into my ear. 'As I'm sure you were – once.'

I sighed theatrically. 'Now you're just being impertinent. A specialist in what, exactly? Needles? Drills? Unnecessary dentalwork?'

'Such things are for the mere amateur,' she murmured.

I felt a sudden movement around my ankles. My shoes were unlaced and then, together with my socks, pulled off. Here it came. What the devil did she have planned for me? Bamboo rammed into the flesh under my toenails? The white-orange flame of a blow-torch?

There was a long, dreadful pause and I tensed myself for the inevitable agony.

Still nothing.

Then I twitched as I felt a sudden bizarre movement on my bare feet. It was a soft, swishing motion, back and forth over the arches and under the toes. It broke off as suddenly as it had started, and Melissa ffawthawte's face appeared right next to mine. From the tiny wrinkling around her green eyes, I could see she was smiling.

In her hand she held something. It was white and, for a moment, my bleary eyes couldn't take in its shape against the glass walls of the room.

A feather!

The silly bitch was tickling me.

'Oh really,' I chortled – and the leather straps groaned again. 'You're not serious?'

The girl sat back a little on the stool. 'My travels have taken me to some interesting places, Mr Box. I long ago discovered that pain and pleasure are but two sides of the same coin. You have no idea how much a man can give away when the core of his soul has been exposed.'

'Or his soles, I suppose,' I chuckled. 'Shame the Inquisition never thought of this lark. I'm sure it would've brightened up the old auto-da-fé no end.'

She shrugged and raised the feather once more.

A tantalising pause and then she resumed her work. I began to titter. Really, what a pleasant way to be tortured! Soon, I was laughing out loud, a delightful tingling running up and down my spine, turning into a warm, fuzzy sensation around the nape of my neck. And then behind my ears.

'This reminds me, *haha* . . .'

Miss ffawthawte's head cocked to one side.

'Barber shops . . . oh, *hahaha*!' I snorted. 'Electrical clippers. Such a pleasant sensation, when the back of one's neck is . . . *heehee* . . . buzzed over.'

Sweat was beading my face and dripping over my lips. I laughed convulsively, from deep inside my chest, and the aged muscles in my sides started to twinge.

And all at once, I realised that I really, really wanted the pleasant sensation to stop.

The tickling, however, continued unabated.

I giggled on, wheezing and coughing as tears sprang to my eyes and coursed over my face, mingling with the salty sweat and pooling in the hollow at the base of my throat.

My toes wriggled involuntarily as I tried desperately to get them away from the feather's touch. I began to arch my back, shrinking from Miss ffawthawte's tender ministrations, but the straps held me tight and my whole body began to shudder.

Then I started screaming. It was too much. Too, too much. Too delightful. I screeched and howled and gasped and laughed and laughed until my lungs heaved. My toes cramped and my legs convulsed, the leather straps cutting horribly into the yielding pink flesh. The sensation had a sort of wonderful horror to it – as though ants were swarming over every inch of my skin, tiny feet caressing each hair. I strained desperately against the leather straps.

'Stop!' I croaked. 'Please. *Please.* Stop!'

The tickling ceased abruptly. Relief washed over me and I took huge, deep breaths. I could hardly see for the tears.

Miss ffawthawte's face appeared like a painted image of the sun. 'Tell me, then. Quickly. Why are you here? What do you know?'

I swallowed, desperate for moisture, then smiled up at her. 'What do I know? My dear lady, we could be here all night!' I tried to clear my parched throat. 'Sir Anthony van Dyck, 1599 to 1641, was court painter to King Charles the First. Born in Antwerp and apprenticed to Hendrick van Balen—'

The girl snarled and began clawing at my shirt. I felt startlingly cold as she ripped it off, exposing my whole naked torso. This time there was no pause and I shrieked as her nails began to scratch and tickle around my armpits. This was worse than the foot torture. Unbidden, memories of long-ago scraps with my brother flashed into my fevered mind. His knees pinning down my arms. The dreadful, unbearable horror of his quick hands tickling at my armpits as I writhed and howled for release.

'Stop, stop, *stop*!' I mewled.

I gasped and sank my teeth into my lip at the terrible loveliness of it all. Blood trickled over my chin but I was scarcely aware of its taste, as waves of ghastly pleasure slammed at my senses. It was unspeakable, sensational, sublime in its horror. I had to stop the tickling or I would go completely mad. Thrashing at my bonds, I yelled and cursed and called ffawthawte every name under the sun.

Now she too was laughing: a crazed, hysterical sound as her talons paddled remorselessly around my armpits. 'Now you'll pay for that little game we played, Mr Box. You'll pay for the humiliation you inflicted on me! Are you dying comfortably?' she shrieked.

Soon, I knew, I would have to tell her everything. That MI6 were on to her organisation. That, even now, a trap was being laid for her.

I howled.

My pulse throbbed in my temple. I could stand no more. My head felt as though it would burst.

Then, unexpectedly, the door shushed smoothly open. 'Desist,' said a quiet voice.

Reluctantly, Melissa ffawthawte sat back on her stool. The relief was glorious, incredible.

'You won't get anything out of Mr Box.' The voice was cold and measured as droplets from an icicle. 'He's one of the old school.'

Stunned almost into unconsciousness, I tried to twist my head to see the newcomer but he remained frustratingly beyond my line of sight.

'What, then?' snapped ffawthawte. 'Shall I shoot him?'

'Oh, no, no, no. Nothing so vulgar. No. We shall be kind to Mr Lucifer Box,' whispered the voice. 'It is time for him to be embraced by the wings of the Black Butterfly . . .'

There was a faint tinkling sound from close by. Then ffawthawte was once more leaning over me. Savagely, she yanked open my mouth, dropped something inside and a bitter taste spread over my tongue.

Almost at once, my head began to swim. But, as I blacked out, one thought began to race around my exhausted brain.

I knew that voice. I knew that voice of old.

It was *Dr Fetch*!

It was the voice of A.C.R.O.N.I.M.!

.15.
LE PAPILLON NOIR

There's a sound. Incessant. Pulsing. Like a drum-roll that doesn't stop.

Eyes open . . .

A great panorama. A cinemascope of water. Mirror blue, then brown, navy and finally cornflower blue as it meets the sky.

Eyes close . . .

I'm numb. Novocaine numb. There's a voice from somewhere. My voice.

Wake up! Wake up! Wake up!

But it's all I can do to lie there. The pulsing pounding beats on and on.

Then there's another sound. Soothing. A crashing, rolling roar. And I can move my head a little. There's sand in my mouth. Rough, salty sand. My eyelids are a closed canopy, pale green, then fiery orange. Sunlight washes over me and it's wonderful. The hairs on my arms rise up.

Eyes open . . .

Firm, golden sand, wind-whipped into ridges. Right by my face, a black beetle is toiling. It looks like a coffee bean. I smile at it.

Blink. A curl of orange peel, speckled with quartzy sand. Matchsticks. A lone vodka bottle, glinting. Broken shells, white as china. A tiny crab gently excavating a hole. Grains of sand stick to its pincers and protuberant eyes. I watch it for some time in sleepy fascination, then roll onto my back.

The pulsing pounding hammers on.

A raw sun, dazzling as a torchbeam. Impossibly blue sky. I screw up my eyes and put out a hand to push myself up. Then the pulsing pounding slams inside my head like a clattering train and I gasp and fall back as though struck. I hit the hot, hard sand and there's no breath in me. I look at my hand. At the hand I reached out with. *And it's not my hand.*

But now the numbness is passing and I sit up and I'm dizzy and the world seems too big and I clamp shut my eyes again until the pulsing and the pounding dies down a little. Just a little. And then I look at my hand again.

Both my hands. Hold them out in front of me. Flip them over and back a dozen times. They're smooth. Pink. Unblemished. They *are* my hands. But yesterday's hands.

Now I use them to slowly, carefully, unbutton my shirt. And they feel strange, as though they're frost-nipped, like when I threw snowballs as a child. There's a palm tree nearby and its shadows dapple me. Now my shirt is off and I'm looking down at my chest. It's a fine chest. Well-muscled. There's a line of black hair like a trail of iron filings leading over the flat stomach to my groin.

And now the pulsing pounding roars in my head and glee grips me and I tear off the rest of my clothes and I stand up. I run my hands over my naked body and face. Everywhere, my fingers meet firm lines, taut muscles. My cheekbones sharp as blades on ice. It's impossible! It's wonderful! And it can't be true . . .

Mirror, mirror, mirror – I have to find a mirror!

I look straight ahead towards the sea. Static clouds echo the fluffy white of the breaking rollers. But there's nothing on the broad beach except me, a few palms and that morning's footprints, softened, rounded by the wind. I take a huge breath. My skin tingles.

Then I run, forgetting all thoughts of mirrors and reflections. Run towards the surf and hurl myself into it and the water is as warm as blood. As the blood that's pulsing and pounding in my head. I roll and dive and wriggle like an otter through its soft embrace. Then I shoot to the surface and the spray bursts over me and I spit out great mouthfuls of salt water. I feel *alive.*

I swim on for what seems like hours and then I'm suddenly exhausted and I slosh up the beach and back onto the sand. The hot, white sand under my high arches. My feet are dusted in fine black hair and they leave impressions in the wet sand that instantly vanish as seawater rises to claim them.

The sun dries me rapidly and then the pulsing pounding returns and I know I have to *get on, get on, get on.* I hurry back into my crumpled shirt and trousers. What the hell should I do next?

I stumble over the dunes, the breeze flapping at my open

shirt. Then I'm suddenly on a long ribbon of pot-holed road and the tarmac is bubbling in the heat. My legs feel strong and lean and long.

A distant rumble but I can't tell if it's thunder or the pulse in my head that keeps urging me *on, on, on.* Then there's a honking sound and I think, *It's a car*, and I turn and a blue dot on the wobbling heat-haze of the horizon resolves itself into a rusty truck. I step out into the road and hold up my arms but the horn blares again and the truck trundles past so I walk on, the hot road scorching my bare soles. Then I turn as another vehicle appears.

It's an open-topped tourer and the driver is an old lady. I smile. She looks like a pig in a wig, her cloud of white hair framed by a huge pink hat. She slows down as she approaches and the breeze flaps at my open shirt and trousers.

She pulls up just by me and drags her white oval sunglasses down the bridge of her snout. A smile tugs at her lips. Her cracked carmine lips. *Hi*, she says, and she drawls it like a record slowing down.

Hello. The word sounds odd in my mouth. It's yesterday's voice. A young voice. *Heading for Kingston?*

Where'd you pitch up from?

I rose from the waves, my love, I hear myself saying. *Like Venus*.

Is that a fact? she chuckles, her flabby neck wobbling. She pats the white seat next to her. *Well, hop in, honey. I could use the company.*

So I get in and the car speeds away and I close my eyes and revel in the glorious feeling of the wind streaming through my long, sleek, jet-black hair. No one has gazed on this particular face since King Bertie died – and now this kindly old dame has me all to herself.

You got business in Kingston? she asks, shifting gear.

Pleasure, I say.

On pleasure bent, huh?

All pleasure should be a little bent, don't you think?

She throws back her head and laughs, then takes one hand off the wheel to stop her sun-hat from flying backwards and then reaches over and squeezes my thigh.

Eyes close . . .

Eyes open . . .

And suddenly we're in the city. She slows down the car and I hop out and turn back to blow her a kiss. She looks awfully disappointed.

I Pause.

There's a bad aching in my joints and muscles because they're new again and need wearing in. The hotel's façade has taken on a peachy glow in the dying sun. It's beautiful. Everything is beautiful. I am beautiful.

The black concierge is still sweating in his too-large uniform, the epaulettes wilting like dead chrysanthemums on his shoulders.

Then the pulsing pounding comes again and it's like an orgasm and I grin with the sheer thrill of it all – my every sense more alert, sharper, quicker.

Then there's a number in my head. Two-oh-nine. Two-oh-nine.

I begin to climb the huge plane tree by the eastern wall of the hotel. The ache is there again but it's lost in the throb of the blood in my head and, with all my long-forgotten agility, I quickly scale the branches. Then I jump from the tree onto a striped awning and get a foothold on the first-floor balcony. From there I clamber up another floor and then another until I'm standing, panting but exhilarated, outside the half-open windows of Kingdom Kum's room.

Muslin curtains flutter. The darkened interior is revealed, then hidden, then revealed. The boy lies dozing on the bed, one arm tucked under his head.

I draw aside the curtain and move towards him, my bare feet soundless on the thick carpet. Kingdom's body is dark against the white counterpane. He's wearing a pair of shorts. That's all. I sit down next to him and gently begin to stroke my hand over his brown legs. He doesn't stir, even as my fingers touch the white soles of his long, bony feet. The pulsing pounding begins to rise again and I feel my hair standing on end. Electricity floods through me. I glance down at him. The dead-straight fall of hair covers one side of his face. A tiny isthmus of spit connects the softness of his slightly parted lips. They're pink as petals.

I move my hands to his waist. The brass button slips easily through the denim and the zip slides down a full inch in response. It's easy work to pull the garment down his legs. He stirs and his lovely features crumple into a grumpy frown, like a child woken from a pleasant dream. But still he sleeps on.

I place my finger on the creamy curve of his backside and score my nail over his skin. He flinches ever so slightly. Then I run my tongue over his hipbone and across the flat washboard of his belly and he makes a gentle little grunting noise, as one of his arms flops over the side of the bed.

His skin tastes warm and slightly salty. He's been in the sea. My tongue trips over his hairless legs and the high arches of his feet. Then I take the little toe of his left foot into my mouth and gently suck it. A lazy half-smile springs to his lips.

Moving up the bed, I nuzzle the dark brown circles of his nipples. They harden and spring to life beneath my teeth. Then my clothes are on the floor and I slide my naked body against Kingdom's.

The warmth of him is like a balm.

His almond-shaped eyes flick open and then they're wide with surprise.

His mouth opens. To cry out? To protest? To welcome?

Then the pulsing and the pounding is like a tidal wave in my head and Miss Beveridge can go hang and I'm Lucifer Box and I'm alive again and I fall upon him like a starving man upon a banquet.

His soft nose bends against my face as my kisses crush him, my cheek is hot against his neck and the delicate curves of his cupped ears. Then I force his arms down onto the counterpane and lick and bite at the dark, hairless pits below. Kingdom writhes, his pretty head twisting back and forth, hair plastered to his forehead. His long, lean legs curl around my hips and he looks up and grins at me; dark lashes beating softly.

Above us, the ceiling fan judders through the sticky air. I'm only distantly aware of the honking of the sluggish traffic in the crowded streets below, and then there's nothing but sweat and spit and my eyes pressed to his and then we're dozing on the destroyed sheets.

Eyes close . . .

At last, the boy opens one lazy eye and tickles his long fingers over my chest.

You're full of surprises, baby, I hear him say, though his voice sounds funny, like a bad connection on the telephone. *What happened to you?*

I got lucky, I say. *You like?*

I like. Good thing I love older men, huh?

I laugh. What is there between us now? Five years? Six? I sit up. Stretch. I feel rested. But not sated. Impossible to be sated now. *I must go on, on, on!*

What now? I say. *What shall we do now?*

Well, in case you've forgotten, lover, I have some bad men to track down.

I wave that away and jump off the bed, throwing open the shutters and letting the orange blaze of the sunset wash over my flesh. *No, no.* We *have to track them down! You and me. Must get on! Run. Swim. No! I did that. Maybe we could go for a drive? Would you like that, Kingdom? Drive down to a casino and lose a pot of money – hm? No, we have to get after Black Butterfly, don't we? Oh! I know something you don't know!*

Kingdom flicks his hair from his burning black eyes and laughs. *Slow down, honey.*

But I don't like the sound of that. I won't hear of that. *Slow down? Why? Why should I? Don't you see what a gift I've been given?*

The boy's face creases in a frown and that's a shame. It's a lovely face. And now I want to kiss it again so I do. Again and again and again and he has to stop me so he can say: *Gift?*

Yes! Come on. Get dressed. We're going for a ride.

Thought we just did.

I slap at his rump and he swears and giggles and then, leaping out of bed, throws his arms around me. *Seriously, baby. You got to go easy . . .*

He looks deep into my eyes and then his face creases again and he says, *Oh God. Not you, too.*

But I'm not listening because, visible through the parted shutters, is a beautiful blue Chevrolet Corvette convertible. It glitters in the light from the ocean. Among the cheap heaps that surround it, it's like a jungle beast. Now there's a new sound joining the pulsing and the pounding – and it's my heart thudding in my ribs. I want it so badly. I must have the car. I wanted the boy and I got him. Now I must have the car.

And then I'm throwing on my shirt and trousers and I tear the room upside down in search of shoes, stupid shoes and at last I come upon a pair of rope sandals and pull them on and I'm at the door. *Come on!*

Kingdom slips back into his tiny denim shorts and rushes after me: *Wait! Wait!*

My sandals make a clapping sound on the marble floors that I find hilarious. The stairs go by, two at a time, and I'm giggling like a child at the wonder of it all. Then I'm through the lobby and the concierge is reading the *Daily Gleaner* and its pages are sun-bleached and he's a stupid idiot to be wasting his life reading about things instead of doing things – like me!

The night. It's warm and beautiful and alive with the chant of insects.

Then Kingdom's hands are on me – but they are no longer a lover's hands. Now they try to pull me back, to constrain me. *Take these! You must take these, baby!* but I push him away. He comes back so I punch him and he goes down.

Then I'm inside the car and trying to start it. The fat concierge is at the window and he says, *What the hell are you doing?* I laugh and laugh and he opens the passenger door and jumps in. Then there's a cloud of dust and scorched rubber and we're thundering onto the main road. *Where? Where? Where?* I shout, and I glance quickly at the man next to me.

The concierge's eyes flicker back and forth. He's nervous. Why? I'm a good driver. A great driver. The best driver. Best in the world, I shouldn't wonder.

Please, he says. *Stop the car, sir. You're crazy.*

I scream with laughter. Crazy? Crazy? I've never felt so good in my life! I throw the car into fourth and ram down my sandalled foot on the accelerator but it's not fast enough. I want my foot to go clean through the floor.

Ahead of us, boxy cars flash by. Ugly, squalid, stupid little cars. I jab the heel of my hand against the horn and the hot evening splits apart with the shrill blast. *Come on!* I yell. *Come on! Out of the blasted way!*

Tail-lights bob and weave ahead like animals' eyes caught in a flashlight, and the highway becomes a kind of tunnel as we tear along, swerving round other vehicles, street lamps blurring, neon advertising signs jumping out of the darkness: smiling girls with toothpaste smiles. And I'm grinning now and my face aches with it and the shrieking laughter that I can't keep down.

And the concierge looks scared stiff and that makes me laugh even more.

Slow down, mister!

The giggle rises in my guts again and then bubbles to my lips. I rock back and forth, back and forth, gripping onto the steering wheel for grim death or grim life, my teeth bared in a rictus of pleasure. And I floor the accelerator because we have to go faster, faster, *faster.*

Houses that are just corrugated roofs glitter in the neon wash. We zip past and I try to overtake a fat Mercedes. Its horn screeches in response. I catch a glimpse of the driver's bleached face and he looks so scared that I laugh again and then swing the Chevy towards him. There's a big crunch and its loudness surprises me but I like the sound so I do it again.

Jesus! screams the concierge. *Pull over, man! Pull over!*

But I ignore him completely. Instead, I swing the car left and then roar back towards the Mercedes. The other car's left headlight explodes into fragments that scree past us like comet dust. I see the driver's face again and it's comical, wildly animated, his mouth jabbering curses at me. He tries to drop back but I don't want to let him, so I grapple with the gears and smash the Chevrolet into him again.

I feel long and lean and brilliant. The concierge is sweating, pale. He grips his seat and screws shut his eyes.

What's the matter? I cry. *It's fun! It's like* Ben Hur*!* Ben HIM*!*

For God's sake, he hisses, and his teeth are clamped together. *You're gonna kill us! You're gonna kill the both of us!*

I shake my head and find I can't stop. The pulsing pounding is like a marching band inside my temples. And the slamming of my heart is hot and furious as lava, coursing through every vein, every sinew.

But then the Mercedes suddenly drops back and I'm totally blind-sided and he hammers into the rear of me. The concierge yelps in panic as we lurch forward and then I'm disappointed because I lose control of the car. I grapple with the dimpled steering wheel but my hands are slick with sweat and the Chevrolet leaps into the oncoming lane. There's a fresh chorus of enraged horns. It's a fanfare. I laugh again.

Oh God – Oh God – Oh God! whines the concierge, clasping his arms around himself as a pair of huge headlights rear up before us. Then there's a stomach-deep thump and then a whiplash that makes me feel sick and we're flung violently to the right and then there's nothing but a skidding swirl as the car spins off the road. Headlights and tail-lights and neon signs and bar signs screw up into fireworks and then the car crunches onto its side and I feel heat as though an oven door has swung open. Then sudden cool and I know I've been thrown clear and . . .

. . . and the light is strange and different and I taste coarse sand in my mouth.

I look around quickly. Distantly, the black ocean glitters

under a half-moon. The Chevrolet is on its side next to a knot of palm trees, flames licking at its rear. I struggle forward on my elbows. My heart is still racing and my mouth is parched. Through the shattered windscreen, I see the concierge, his head lolling on his chest, and I know he's dead.

But I don't care about him. Why should I? I have to get going. And the pulsing pounding is like thunder, blocking out all other sounds.

I drag myself under some palms just as the fire takes hold and the car explodes. I turn my face away from the fierce orange flame and then I hear another car. It screams across the beach and Kingdom Kum gets out and runs over to me. Then his long fingers are on my mouth and something bitter is dropped on my tongue and he's forcing me to swallow. But I'm not interested in him because I see something that doesn't make sense. In the hard, white sand is one of the Chevrolet's wing mirrors. It's cracked in two but in the moonlight and the glow from the wreck, my own face is reflected back. And it's the face of an old man.

.16.
WHO LOOKS INSIDE, AWAKENS

A man with an unkempt moustache was shining a pencil-thin beam of light in my eyes. I could see nothing except him, pooled in darkness. I recoiled, then realised that his thumb was holding open my eyelid. I cursed him – his fingers stank of nicotine – and then there was a hand on my arm and a voice: 'Easy, baby. *Easy*.'

Then sleep crashed over me like the surf on the bone-white Kingston sand.

I turned over, hot and anxious, the bedsheets too tight, swaddling me. I cried out and then felt a hand on my jaw again, but this time a gentle, cool hand. I tasted the same bitterness in my mouth, though this was assuaged immediately by a drink of water. It spilled over my chin and onto my chest, but I didn't care about that. Sleep dragged me down once more.

I felt a bar of sunlight on my face and was suddenly awake. I took in the iron-framed bed, the white-walled room, the ridiculous pyjamas into which I'd been decanted.

Kingdom Kum, searching me with wide-open eyes, sat opposite.

'Hey,' he said.

I blinked.

'How're you feeling?'

I rubbed a hand over my bristly chin. I felt ancient, fragile as a disinterred mummy, and my muscles were weak. I remembered the feeling from my schooldays. Trying to button my shirt after a freezing cross-country run. Hands too numb. Why was I thinking about school?

'Where am I?' I said at last.

'Private hospital in Kingston.'

I shivered inside my pyjamas, muscles throbbing, hamstrings aching. 'Lovely place,' I murmured. I felt my eyes roll in my head and made an effort to focus. 'Kingston-upon-Thames. Leafy. Very leafy. Hm?'

Kingdom Kum got up and poured a glass of water. 'You don't remember what happened?'

I took the water and then noticed my own trembling hand. My delicate, veiny, age-spotted hand. 'I know you, don't I?' I said, smiling at the boy. He nodded. 'And there was something about butterflies. I'm rather fond of butterflies.' I drank some of the water.

Kingdom Kum looked worried.

I shivered again and closed my eyes, fragments of memory spangling and flaring in my mind's eye like a shaken kaleidoscope. I thrust the glass back at the boy, fighting down the sensation.

'It's okay, baby,' soothed Kingdom. 'Take it easy.' He stroked the hair back off my forehead. 'Thought I'd never catch you. I got the antidote into you just in time.' He took a glass tube from his pocket and rattled it. 'I liberated them from the clinic, remember?'

I shook my head and laughed. 'You had me worried back there. I thought we were gonna lose you.'

'I didn't know you cared,' I said. 'Oh, that was very rude of me. Why am I being rude to you? You're very, very pretty.'

'I couldn't tell you who I was working for, baby—'

I grinned stupidly. 'No?'

'No. Orders from the top. I was to keep you out of trouble. Gently encourage you to quit the field.' Kingdom beamed suddenly, wonderfully. 'But there ain't no stopping the great Lucifer Box, is there?'

'I expect not!' I cried. Then: 'Who's Lucifer Box?' My mind clouded again and I sipped at the water like a child.

'You saw Mr Playfair – you remember that?'

I shook my head. Then nodded, eagerly. 'Playfair, yes. Yes, I know someone of that name.'

'And then where did you go?'

I frowned, trying desperately to remember. I knew I wanted to please the young man. He was extremely alluring. But nothing came. Nothing except the sweet sensation of the pulsing blood in my temples, the rush of adrenalin and a beautiful car that I was urging on and on and on . . .

'I remember a Chevrolet.' I looked over at the boy, and the soft line of his neck and jaw brought back other, even sweeter sensations. 'And I remember you.' I winked at him. 'Fancy a fuck?'

The boy laughed, then looked down, eyelashes beating a slow tattoo.

I held out my hands before me. 'It's such a shame I'm so old, my dear boy. You're a looker and then some. My God, in my day . . .' I trailed off. 'Funny, but somehow it doesn't seem that long ago. *Young.* Vital. So alive!'

Kingdom leaned forward and took my hand. 'It wasn't so long ago, baby.'

I pushed him away. 'No pity, please.'

'No, man. You were on fire! You came to me and I wanted you,' persisted Kingdom. 'It was cool.'

I sniggered. 'You're kidding.'

'I mean it! It doesn't matter how old you are. I *like* you.'

I shrugged. What was the boy talking about? 'Butterflies,' I said suddenly. 'I wish I was a butterfly. In a chrysalis.' I gave a little sigh. 'A Black Butterfly.'

The door clicked open to reveal a smiling man. He was dressed in an absurdly colourful shirt and colonial shorts. His milk-white knees were as knobbly as golf balls.

'Oh!' I cried. 'It's Mr Playfair, isn't it? I was just telling my young friend here that I knew someone of that name.'

'Hello, old love,' said the newcomer, frowning. 'How're you feeling?'

'Fine,' I said. 'How long have I been here, Mr Playfair?'

He dropped into a chair and crossed his legs. 'Just a day. Probably feels like a lifetime, eh?'

I clamped shut my eyes; my addled mind felt as if it was awash with soup. 'I wish I could remember,' I tutted, thumping the side of my head in frustration. 'Why can't I remember?'

Playfair exchanged a worried look with Kingdom Kum and then patted the bedclothes. 'Listen, old love. You mustn't think about all that. You've been in the wars, and according to Mr Kum here, you were ruddy lucky to escape unscathed. I think it's time we got you home.'

I sat up, sharply. 'What?'

'Look, Box, old man, you've done more than enough. Terrific service to King and country. Queen and country too! It's time to let it go, old love. Now . . .' he opened his jacket and pulled out a rectangle of paper '. . . first class back to Blighty. What do you say?'

I stared at him, mouth agape, desperately trying to order my muddled thoughts. 'Home?' I said. 'Yes. That would be lovely.'

'Good!' cried Playfair. 'Excellent!'

I hardly noticed as he rose and went to the door.

Kingdom Kum crossed to the bed and sat down on it. 'There's no shame in calling it a day, baby.'

I shut my eyes and sank back on the pillow. 'Very tired now. Wish I could remember, but . . .'

Playfair came back in, and I opened my eyes. Two young men of about eighteen were trotting dutifully behind him. Blond and fit, they were in some kind of uniform. Long khaki shorts and socks, broad-brimmed hats hanging on a string behind their backs.

'Hello!' I called gaily. 'Who are you?'

'This is Heathcoat,' Playfair told me, slowly, as though addressing a child. 'And this is Amory. They're part of Lord Battenburg's personal security team. But I don't suppose you remember any of that?'

Then, all of a sudden, everything was clear. My faculties snapped back into place like an elastic band.

'Oh my God!' I yelled. 'That's it! That's *it*!'

Playfair frowned. 'That's what?'

I stared at the newcomers. 'They're his bodyguard? Battenburg's bodyguard?'

Playfair nodded. 'Part of it. Sends just the right message, don't you think? Twenty strapping young men from different nations. What could be better? I say, old love, you're sounding more like your old self!'

I rubbed my hand over my face and tried to get out of bed but a wave of wooziness overwhelmed me.

'Hey, baby,' said Kingdom, reaching towards me. 'Slow down.'

I pushed him angrily away. My mind was clearing all the time. 'The New Scout Movement! Melissa ffawthawte!' I shouted. 'They're the front for A.C.R.O.N.I.M.!'

Playfair chuckled. 'Now steady on, old love.'

'Don't patronise me, Playfair,' I snapped. 'It's coming back to me. It's all coming back to me. You have to listen!'

'You're not well,' said Playfair sternly.

Heathcoat and Amory gazed down at me, icy-blue eyes giving nothing away.

'Playfair,' I said, patiently, '*Allan.* My son is here in Jamaica. Attending the New Scout Movement's Great Jamboree . . .'

'Good. Excellent. Glad to see you've got the lad on the right track.'

'Listen!' I hissed. 'Just listen!' I put my hands to my temples, struggling to focus. 'After . . . after I left you in the hotel, I went down to try and see him. Yes – that's right. While I was there, I met a woman I'd last seen at a Scout camp back in England.'

'Surely no surprise there?'

'She had a tattoo, Playfair. On her breast! A Black Butterfly. I was knocked out—'

'I'm not surprised,' chuckled Playfair.

I glared at him. 'Then I was tortured. And then there was a voice! The voice of Dr Fetch! The whole New Scout Movement is a cover for A.C.R.O.N.I.M. They're back!'

'A.C.R.O.N.I.M.?' scoffed Playfair, shaking his head. 'Get a ruddy grip, old love. Sooner we send you back home, the better.'

'Why would I lie?' I turned to Kingdom and grabbed at him. '*You* must believe me! Surely you believe me, Kingdom?'

But the boy just looked helplessly at me. I could see the doubt and confusion in his almond-shaped eyes.

Playfair sighed. 'No one's suggesting you're lying, Box. You're just a little confused. Not surprising after what you've been through, is it?'

'You insufferable idiots!' I roared. 'You think you've got this whole situation controlled. Down pat! But there's more to it. The Scouts—'

Playfair held out his hands, palms upward. 'I understand. I really do. You can't bear the idea of packing it all in. And then somebody fed you that bloody awful narcotic and you've got things all upside down.'

'Yes!' I cried. 'Someone did feed me the drug. A.C.R.O.N.I.M.!'

Playfair shot a pleading look at Kingdom Kum who just shrugged. 'In your mind,' he said, 'you've made up this story, resurrecting the great enemy of your heyday.'

'It's all true, damn you!' I glared up at the bland, imperturbable faces of the Scouts. 'And what's more,' I spat out, 'they know it.'

'Now that's enough,' barked Playfair. 'I've been more than indulgent with you out of respect for your position. But this really is the limit.'

I shot a last appealing look to Kingdom Kum as Playfair turned to Heathcoat and Amory. 'Escort Mr Box to the airport, would you, boys? He has a plane to catch.' He tossed over the airline ticket. 'One way.'

.17.
THE MAN WITH THE CELLULOID HAND

I sweltered in the leathery stink of the vehicle, squeezed uncomfortably between the twin Scouts Heathcoat and Amory. A third Scout, Mexican and as impassive as his fellows, was driving. The city rolled by, serene and ordinary. Just another warm Kingston evening, the harsh chirrup of the cicadas in the monkeyfiddle trees, the sun going to its scarlet ocean grave.

But my mind was racing. *Fetch was alive!*

It was incredible, impossible! Yet, as I'd succumbed to the wretched Black Butterfly, I'd recognised his voice. I would know those arctic tones anywhere, even after all these years. But how could my Nemesis have survived?

In my mind's eye, I saw again the slender, elegant frame in velvet frockcoat, the sparse, straw-like hair, the cold, bleak eyes. And the hand, of course, fashioned from celluloid, clicking mechanically as Fetch wrapped his digits about my neck . . .

This, though, was not the time for reflection. I risked a look at my captors, their brawny bodies pressed against my sides.

The Scouts should have looked absurd, hulking great brutes in silly uniforms, but their muscular frames and grim, set faces brooked no argument.

I sighed. Playfair had been completely duped. A.C.R.O.N.I.M. wouldn't have to worry about getting past Lord Battenburg's security. A.C.R.O.N.I.M. *were* his security!

Minutes ticked by. We passed rusty cars drawn up outside apartment blocks, their blue shadows lengthening; phone booths like bars of gold, glinting with the last of the sunshine. I kept my own counsel, staring down at Heathcoat's huge red knees, unsure as to whether the Scouts would follow through Playfair's orders and deliver me to the airport, or whether they had a nice little detour planned: ending with a bullet in the back of my neck.

If only Kingdom Kum had believed my rambling story! But, no. Once again, I was on my own.

A sign for the airport flashed by. This was my last throw.

'Might I smoke?' I asked.

Amory, on my left, only shrugged and tossed his blond fringe from his narrow eyes. I reached for my cigarette case but his burly chum grabbed my hand. 'I'll get that,' said Heathcoat.

He slipped his hand inside my jacket and pulled out the battered old fag case.

'Thanks,' I said, grinning foolishly. 'Bit shaky, to be honest. Not nice to have Mr Playfair tell one off, eh?'

The boy grunted and busied himself lighting my cigarette.

'You know,' I continued, 'I didn't mean all that guff about your lovely Movement. You do realise that, don't you?'

Still no response. I looked him quickly up and down. Was he armed? Did Scouts carry knives? But then these were hardly ordinary Scouts. Heathcoat might well be packing a Walther P38 inside his jockey shorts for all I knew. The burly creature took a long, self-satisfied drag on the cigarette, then passed it over. I took it with a trembling hand.

I drew on it and as I did so, feigned a violent spasm of coughing, bringing down my elbows sharply onto the webbed belt that ran around the inside of my trousers. At once, I felt Whitley Bey's emergency rehydration packs rupture and begin to bleed out onto the cloth.

Amory noticed at once and smiled.

I gave a little wail of distress and glanced down at my crotch. 'Oh God! Oh no . . .'

Both Scouts looked down at my crotch and horrid little grins crept across their smooth young faces.

I closed my eyes in despair. 'Oh Christ. How shaming.'

'Hur-hur,' chortled Amory. 'He's bleedin' wet hisself.'

'Wet hisself,' chimed Heathcoat.

I gestured helplessly. 'I'm so sorry. The . . . the smell and sweat of my trousers,' I said, 'is nauseating at three in the afternoon.'

Instinctively, the Scouts drew away from me. It was all the chance I needed. With all my strength, I threw a punch and got Amory under the firm line of his jaw, my knuckles cracking like tinder in a bonfire. His square head rammed into the window and he fell back at once, out cold.

The car swerved.

Immediately, I swung over and chopped the edge of my

hand into Heathcoat's windpipe. The lad rasped in agony. Spit flew from his snarling mouth and he flung his weight onto me, but I managed to get the heel of my hand up and smashed it into his nose. Blood gushed down his tawny shirt. He roared in fury and tried to get his hands round my throat but I was all over him, scrabbling for any kind of weapon. Suddenly my fingers fell on a knife, the fleur-de-lys design on the hilt flashing in the last embers of sunlight.

Heathcoat tried to twist out of the way but I jabbed the dagger towards his face.

'No!' he yelped. 'Don't! For God's sake—'

Without further ado, I grabbed hold of his blond locks and smacked his head against the window. The tinted glass was suddenly bright with blood and he rolled over to join his friend in the Land of Nod.

The car veered again alarmingly and I saw the Mexican driver's startled eyes in the mirror as he took in the chaotic scene. 'Pull up!' I shouted, jabbing the knife at the back of his neck as though pricking a sausage. 'Now! *Now!*'

He screeched over to the side of the road and slammed on the brakes. The car mounted the pavement and collided with a road sign, the bonnet wrapping itself around the rusty pole like a concertina. I fell forward but managed to whack the Mexican on the back of the head with the hilt of the dagger and he collapsed over the wheel. The car was a write-off.

I took a panting, excited breath and clambered out. It was, I knew, all a matter of self-belief. The things I'd done when I'd thought myself young again! My whole body might ache, shriek its aged protest – but it was possible, it was all possible!

If I could just get to the Summit in time . . .

Night had closed like a fox-stole over the city. I jogged as swiftly as I could along the hot black road, thinking of what Kingdom Kum had said. I still *had* it!

I turned my step towards the brand new conference centre that I had passed only forty-eight hours before. Thanks to Kingdom's espionage, I knew this was where A.C.R.O.N.I.M. intended to strike. Allan Playfair might be smugly complacent that no one could possibly attack Lord Battenburg, but I knew better. Dr Cassivelaunus Fetch was capable of anything.

As I walked swiftly along, I thought back to the strangely muted end of our long-running duel. Back in 1908, A.C.R.O.N.I.M. had launched Operation Sikh and Destroy – an audacious scheme to use mesmerised Sepoys to assassinate the Viceroy. Though I'd thwarted them, as I'd thwarted them so often before, Fetch himself had eluded me. Until, that is, I'd found him, cowering and wounded, inside a Maharajah's knicker closet.

After that, the Royal Academy had taken him into custody with a promise from the then Joshua Reynolds (little fellow – remember him?) that Fetch's fate would be a fitting one. And yet there had been no great trial, no proper reckoning for the death and destruction A.C.R.O.N.I.M. had wrought. Some months later, I'd simply heard that Fetch had passed away in some grim asylum for the criminally insane.

But I had heard his voice. Fetch lived!

I snapped out of my reverie. I was hot, sweaty, exhausted and without a dollar to my name. But there was no other option than to keep on going, half-running, half-stumbling until the conference centre suddenly loomed up out of the night like a great beach ball: its exterior floodlit, the palm trees that ringed the place waving in the soft breeze. Tonight, the leaders of the free world would be assembled there. God only knew how he intended to do it, but there was no doubt in my mind that Fetch was the architect of this murderous campaign.

I stole around the perimeter of the conference centre, keeping well away from the floodlit driveway, and then lost myself in the scrubby bushes that occupied the lower slopes of the surrounding hillsides. The driveway bristled with dozens of burly, suited men, whispering into radio sets, suspicious-looking bulges under their armpits. Madly athletic Americans, their white teeth dazzling even from where I was crouching, stood out, but my distinguished successor was nowhere to be seen.

I had to keep a cool head. As Mr Playfair had made abundantly clear, no one was likely to believe my story about the New Scout Movement. Yet, if I failed to act, they were certain to strike Battenburg down.

And then I saw my opportunity. A little to my left, going almost unnoticed because of all the hoo-hah out front, stood a flotilla of trucks. From it issued a steady stream of tuxedoed men, hefting crates, bottles and crockery. Caterers! Thank God!

I glanced down at my ruined black suit and said a silent prayer of thanks that I was still wearing it – purely for the wonderful anonymity it provided. Over my long career, I have extricated myself from many a tricky predicament just by acting as if I own the place. So I simply stood up, hoped no one would notice the absence of a dicky-bow in my ensemble, and joined the queue of waiters, picking up a crate of plonk and passing inside completely undetected.

Whistling insouciantly, I carried the crate through into a starkly white kitchen. Once my cargo had been clattered down, I slipped through a side door into a gloomy, scarcely completed maintenance corridor, thick with wiring.

The distant murmur of voices caught my attention at once and, gripping hold of cold, metal banisters, I climbed a stained concrete staircase – two, three, four floors – until I came to a thick steel door. The buzz of conversation here was much louder.

Carefully I turned the handle and opened the door just a fraction, gaze darting up and down as I tried to drink in all the details with which the narrow strip of light furnished me.

I was standing at the very top of a vast steel dome, lights twinkling in its ceiling like captured stars. Pushing the door open, I stepped out onto one of the narrow gantries that ringed the dome.

Far below, long, semi-circular tables had been erected, behind which the delegates were beginning to take their seats. The bespectacled, green-uniformed Chinese. The smooth-faced Americans. The grim-looking Russians with their iron-grey hair, bad teeth and even worse suits. And, yes, there was the British contingent: the dependable old PM, fat as a Buddha in his pinstripe, casually making small talk with the sun-tanned, distinguished – and doomed – Lord Battenburg.

Before the delegates' tables was grouped a ring of bulky television cameras of the type I'd once seen at Ally Pally during the heady climax of the Bakelite Gorilla Stranglings. These cameras were unmanned, however; bolted into place, pointed at a spot-lit dais. Curiously, close by the cameras was ranged an enormous bank of television *sets*, humming gently, their oval screens currently showing nothing but some kind of geometrical test-card.

I was puzzled. The cameras I could understand. The opening ceremony was to be broadcast across the world. But why the individual sets? Was there to be some kind of transmission for the benefit of the assembled delegates?

Encircling the round room were the New Scout bodyguard, the buttons on their uniforms shiny as gold nuggets. I counted eighteen burly young men, of various races, unsmiling to a man. Their hair was neatly parted, their arms at their sides. Patient as snakes. Allan Playfair – looking immensely self-important – stood nearby. His eyes narrowed as he scrutinised the ceiling. What the hell was he expecting? Ninja warriors to descend from the roof armed with poisonous jam butties?

What could I do? If I tried to warn Lord Battenburg, Playfair would have me carted off again. If I tried to disrupt the ceremony, the Scout bodyguard might strike elsewhere. My God, for all I knew, they were slipping the Black Butterfly to his Lordship right now!

I looked down again at the Scouts and frowned. Playfair had said there would be twenty of them. I'd accounted for three in the car. So why were there eighteen remaining? I peered myopically at the youths but they remained little more than a multi-racial blur of shorts and woggles. Damn my failing eyes!

I was about to move forward on the gantry when I became horribly aware of a presence behind me.

'Well, well, well,' came a purring, contralto voice. 'You're like the proverbial bad penny, aren't you, Mr Box? Now, I'd like you to turn round and face me very, very slowly.'

I did as I was instructed, and stared, not only into the face of the lethally lovely Melissa ffawthawte, but also the barrel of a .357 Magnum.

The girl was dressed in the deceptively conservative garb of the New Scout Movement, a yellow neckerchief around her pale throat, a buff skirt clinging to her shapely hips and thighs. I was once again reminded of that lovely young thing I'd met on Armistice Night. What *was* her name? I flashed ffawthawte my most disarming smile and said: 'I must warn you that if you attempt to tickle me again, I shall be very cross.'

She cocked her head to one side. 'I underestimated you. None of our victims has yet managed to survive the exquisite delights of Black Butterfly. I should be most interested to hear how you succeeded in regaining your sanity.'

'And I'd love to tell you,' I replied. 'Perhaps over dinner. Do you have anything on tonight? It's a lovely evening.'

A mocking smile curled at ffawthawte's minutely scarred lip. 'I'm afraid we both have an appointment, Mr Box. A most pressing appointment.'

She gestured ahead with the Magnum and, putting up my hands, I looked down, but the various occupants of the room were far too preoccupied to notice an elderly waiter and a Scout mistress making their way along a gantry thirty-odd feet above them.

We continued our vertiginous progress around the perimeter of the dome, until Miss ffawthawte ordered me to stop by another narrow door. Keeping the gun trained on me, she leaned over and pushed it open.

The high-ceilinged room beyond resembled some species of Modernist cathedral of the type city councils had been lately throwing up to replace the Gothic beauties flattened by the Luftwaffe. Huge arched windows looked down onto the hall below, and comfortable-looking black chairs were positioned alongside them. Against one wall stood a bank of television screens just like the ones in the main chamber. Otherwise the room appeared to be empty.

'Take a seat, Mr Box,' instructed the girl.

I did so, feigning an indifference I did not truly feel.

'And now?' I asked.

Miss ffawthawte adjusted her steel spectacles and chuckled. 'Now it's time for you to meet the leader of the New Scout Movement; the man who has revived A.C.R.O.N.I.M. and the *genius* who will be responsible for unleashing the power of Black Butterfly upon the world!'

A chill passed through my body. At last, the time had come.

Out of the corner of my eye, I glimpsed a movement. The furthest chair in the row, some eleven or twelve along from the place I occupied, slowly revolved. I took a deep breath as I prepared once more, and after nearly fifty years, to behold my greatest foe.

But sitting on the shiny black leather was not Dr Fetch.

'Christmas!' I cried, astonished.

And there he was, my own son, resplendent in a brand new Scout uniform, his shoes almost as shiny as his glossy black hair, his hands folded neatly in his lap.

'What the hell is this?' I demanded of ffawthawte.

There was a sibilant giggle from close by. I whirled round. Then the voice came, slightly muffled as though passing through a loudspeaker. 'You'll forgive my little joke, I'm sure, Mr Box,' said ffawthawte.

'What the blazes do you think you're doing? Using a child—'

'Not just any child,' she chuckled.

I turned to face Christmas. His little eyes were shining fever-bright. 'Listen to me, son,' I said. 'Everything's going to be fine. I'll get you away from here, don't you worry.'

Christmas turned to ffawthawte, his lip jutting. 'But I'm needed here, aren't I? I'm a very important young man.'

'Of course you are, my darling,' cooed the girl. 'Why don't you be a good boy, Christmas, and tell your daddy what you've learned, eh?'

My son's dark eyes flashed and he grinned. Dimly, I became aware of an introductory speech beginning below us: '*unique technical achievement*'; '*link up tonight's proceedings with Scout huts all across the globe*.'

'On my honour . . . I will do my best' intoned Christmas, sitting up straight on the padded chair. 'To do my duty to the Akela and my fellows and to obey the new Scout law . . .'

Miss ffawthawte nodded encouragingly at him. 'Go on! Go on!'

'To harm the weak all the time,' said Christmas, puffing out his little chest. 'And to do my level best to destroy the pantomime of Western democracy.'

'Excellent!' said ffawthawte. 'Excellent! A special badge for that, I think.'

Christmas laughed and pointed to the emblems embroidered on his sleeve. 'I've done ever so well, Daddy,' he said to me. 'This one's for arson, this one's for strangling kittens and this one—'

My throat tightened with rage. 'My God, you just wait until I get you home—'

'But I'm not coming home. It's much more fun here.'

ffawthawte placed her hand on my son's shoulder, even as she kept her revolver trained on me. I looked into my only child's eyes – and he returned my gaze with the impassivity of a stranger.

'You see, Mr Box,' purred the girl. 'Christmas is our final triumph! Your son belongs to the Movement, body and soul!'

I started as a soft giggle sounded from behind the panelled walls. The hair on my neck rose, as though caressed by the touch of a tarantula. 'Fetch!' I snarled. 'Is that you? Still skulking about in the shadows? Show yourself!' I thumped the arm of the chair. 'Or daren't you face me?'

For answer, the wall glided back with a soft whirr and a figure stepped into the room.

I sat back in the chair, astonished. It *still* wasn't Dr Fetch. It was another child – stumpy-legged, aspirin-white with hollow, burning, hate-filled eyes. Of course – I'd seen him before! It was the weird, sickly-looking creature I had glimpsed watching me through the window at the Scout camp!

But as I looked more closely, I realised that this was no boy. The shrivelled skin, the stunted, dwarfish demeanour – even the coiled curls of yellow hair more resembled the sparse tresses of an old man.

He minced over to where Melissa ffawthawte stood, covering me with the Magnum.

'Mr Box,' he said. 'At last we meet.'

The voice! It *was* Fetch's voice! I looked quickly around. What was this? A ventriloquist act? Was he some kind of doll?

'Or should I say, we meet *properly*,' he went on. 'I had the pleasure of getting close to you in the Hagia Sophia.'

I frowned, baffled. 'What?'

'Of course, you were rather preoccupied at the time . . .'

Suddenly, recent memories screed through my mind like unspooling film. Istanbul . . . The balcony of the Hagia Sophia . . . The press of tourists behind me . . . The little blond boy in the red jumper . . .

I stared at the withered homunculus before me.

'Imagine my delight,' he continued in those all too familiar tones, 'when I saw the great Lucifer Box leaning so precariously, so temptingly above the abyss! Actually, I'm rather glad you survived. You deserve a far more lingering and exquisite death.'

'You pushed me? But why? Who – *what* the hell are you?'

Miss ffawthawte saw the confusion on my face and smiled. 'Mr Lucifer Box,' she said. 'May I introduce you to Cassivelaunus Fetch.'

'Eh?' I cried.

She paused theatrically. '*Junior*.'

.18.
CHILDREN'S HOUR

I have to admit that, in spite of the clear danger I found myself in, I burst out laughing. What a joke, to have been convinced that the most warped being ever to stalk the earth had been somehow resurrected . . .

'Fetch actually managed to produce a sprog?' I asked incredulously. 'What a horrible thought. And you've been reviving the family business, have you? Good for you. Nice to see a bit of gumption amongst the young.' I looked closer at the goblin-like creature. 'But no, you're not young, are you? You'll forgive me for asking, I'm sure, but is there something wrong with you?'

Fetch Junior's watery eyes flickered from side to side. 'An accident of birth,' he snarled.

'Accident?'

My captor hissed, as though physically wounded. 'You cannot begin to imagine the torments my father suffered after you handed him over to your *superiors*. Did they ever tell you? Did they ever reveal to you his ultimate punishment?'

'Must've slipped their minds. But, you know, it can get very busy in the office—'

'They treated him as a human guinea pig!' growled the dwarf. 'He was sent to a dismal asylum. There he became part of a scheme to determine the effects of a new drug that the British Government was developing as a weapon of war.'

'Ah,' I said. 'I see.'

'And when they had broken him,' continued the etiolated midget, 'when the Black Butterfly had ravaged him and he was no more than a shell of the great man he had once been, there was no one left to care. No one except—'

'Your mummy?' I needled. 'What was she? A charlady? Or did she come to the loony bin to slop out the chamber-pots?'

He smacked a papery hand across my face.

I rubbed at my cheek and nodded slowly. 'So that's it. The drug caused birth defects as well! No wonder they broke off the testing. A drug like that in the wrong hands . . .'

A chilling giggle escaped from Fetch Junior's flaky lips. He stretched his palms out towards me. 'Do you know what these are?'

'What?'

'The wrong hands!'

He began to strut up and down before me. 'But if my body is permanently stunted,' he crowed, 'my mind has grown exponentially! I have outdone my father in brilliance.'

'Now, now,' I tutted. 'Nobody likes a show-off.'

'The rediscovery of Black Butterfly – all my work! The

systematic elimination of those invertebrates who developed it – all my work!'

I grimaced in disgust. 'You killed them all?'

He nodded eagerly. 'Gobetween, Meddler, Watchbell and, of course, that fine hypocrite, Sir Vyvyan Hooplah.'

Melissa ffawthawte managed to tear herself away from looking at Christmas and said: 'He was the one who tipped us off as to the origins of the drug. A.C.R.O.N.I.M. had been trying for years to revive Black Butterfly. All the records were supposed to have been destroyed. Hooplah came to our rescue. It seems some public servants will do anything for a price. Unfortunately for him, passing on such top secret information does rather leave one open to blackmail . . .'

So that was how they had lured the old fool to the *Blood Orange* that night! And then I remembered that Boy Scout with the collecting tin. I'd been so convinced that Kingdom Kum had been behind the murder that I'd forgotten all about the wretched kid. And all it would take was a casually dropped pill in the old politician's drink . . .

'And what about Christopher Miracle?' I yelled. 'What had he done to hurt you?'

Fetch smiled. 'Oh, Mr Box, you have been naïve. Don't you see – even now? Oh, well.' He crossed over to Christmas and patted the boy on the head. 'It is rather fitting that you, my father's greatest enemy, should be here to witness his final triumph.'

Fetch pulled himself up to his inconsiderable height and puffed out his spindly chest. 'Because, you see, I am not merely my father's son. I AM AKELA!'

I sighed, feigning boredom. 'Really, *boasting* again. You'll be sent to bed without any supper. Actually, I wanted to ask you about that. Taking over an entire youth movement – all those raffles and sack-races – seems a very roundabout way of getting to Lord Battenburg.'

Fetch Junior and Melissa ffawthawte turned to regard each other. The woman's husky laugh joined with the high-pitched giggle of her colleague. 'Oh Mr Box,' she said. 'Whatever gave you that idea?'

'Come on. As we're being painfully honest with one another, you may as well admit it. There's nothing I don't know already, after all.'

The two continued to appraise me in silent amusement.

'Your final target!' I prompted. 'The man whose discovery of the wretched *papilio obscurus* set all this in motion. *Lord Battenburg!*'

Still nothing.

'It won't work, you know,' I insisted. 'MI6 are watching him like hawks. Tasters check everything he is due to eat or drink. There's no way you can slip the drug to him. Not today. Not ever.'

Fetch Junior shook his little head pityingly. Then Melissa ffawthawte bent down and gave him a long and passionate kiss, his cracked and angry mouth clamping over hers like the sucker of an octopus. It was quite the most revolting thing I've ever seen.

With Christmas between them, they stood there like some absurd parody of a family photograph. Then Fetch broke from the embrace and crept over to the windows, looking down onto the huge delegates' chamber.

'Now I fear I must leave you,' he said, with mock regret. 'I have an appointment of my own to attend to.' He made his way to the far side of the room, and the twin doors of a lift, cleverly concealed within the room's décor, hissed open. The dreadful little thing stepped inside. 'Enjoy the show.'

And he was gone.

Melissa ffawthawte turned to me. 'Dear me, Mr Box. You do look peaky. Has all this been a bit of a shock?'

'What does he mean,' I demanded, valiantly attempting to rally myself, '"enjoy the show"?'

'Tell him, Christmas.'

The sole inheritor of my family name gazed at me calmly. 'Lord Battenburg is going to make a speech,' he began, 'and Akela is going to present him with a special award from the New Scout Movement. Isn't that right, Miss?'

Miss ffawthawte purred her approval. 'That's right, sweetheart. Akela is going to raise a toast to his Lordship: one that will be witnessed by millions of people all across the world. Millions of parents and children, all gathered together in the premises of the New Scout Movement, celebrating, eagerly watching, and ready to drink to the health of Lord Battenburg.'

Her green eyes glittered at me. I was obviously missing something. Something crucial.

'Sharp as a tack, I see,' said the girl. 'Now, please be quiet whilst I switch on the television.'

She moved across to the bank of screens that duplicated the ones set up in the dome below and activated the nearest one.

A small dot appeared on the television. After a moment, it widened until a bluey image of the domed chamber appeared. I watched in fascination. What were A.C.R.O.N.I.M. up to?

I could hear my heart thumping in my ribs. On the screen, I saw the Jamaican delegate banging his gavel. The chattering fell silent. I gritted my teeth and watched helplessly as Lord Battenburg, benevolent and beaming, walked to the dais.

The applause was fulsome and sincere. Even the Russians managed a smile.

'My friends, colleagues, distinguished guests,' he began, gripping his lapels. 'It is with great pride and humility that I welcome you here to Jamaica for this inaugural World Government Summit. It certainly hasn't been easy assembling everybody . . .'

A ripple of polite laughter. I swivelled my gaze briefly towards Christmas and the girl.

'. . . but now we're all here, I do hope we can create a lasting framework for global peace. None of us wants to return to, nor create anew, the circumstances that led to the last war. Here, under the Caribbean sun, we can make a fresh start.'

A torrent of applause from the delegates. Miss ffawthawte was enraptured.

'But you will forgive me, I hope, a little indulgence,' Battenburg went on. He adjusted his position on the dais. One of the Scouts moved his arm and I tensed, but he was only scratching his nose.

'For some time,' continued his Lordship, 'I have kept a project very close to my heart: the New Scouting Movement.'

Applause broke out once more.

Battenburg nodded his approval. 'A Movement which has done so much to inspire our young people. To succour them. To give them a brighter tomorrow. They have even been so farsighted as to make me their Honorary President.'

Laughter from the delegates. Lord Battenburg grinned like a cat.

On the screen, Fetch Junior was suddenly standing close by, ready to join Battenburg on the platform. But what the hell was he planning to do? Battenburg, like some idiot choir-master, began to intone the Scout oath. 'On my honour, I will do my best to do my duty to God and my country . . .'

And then, the tiniest hint of deliverance! My hand brushed over my trouser leg and I felt a small, solid object, forgotten in the depths of my left-hand pocket . . .

'To keep myself physically strong,' continued Battenburg. 'Mentally awake and morally straight . . .'

Now Melissa ffawthawte was joining in with the oath, standing beside me, her voice rising in fervour. 'A Scout looks on the bright side of things,' she cried. 'He cheerfully does tasks that come his way . . .'

Jubilant in the midst of her ranting, she took her eyes off me for the first time and inadvertently lowered the nose of the revolver.

I took a deep breath. It seemed insane. Ridiculous. But it

was the only weapon I had. Of course, it was all a question of angles. Miss ffawthawte had been quite right.

'He does not hurt or kill harmless things without reason,' she cried, then burst out laughing. Her lovely face split into a grin of horrid glee. 'Well, two out of three isn't bad!'

I moved like lightning, snatched the cube of snooker chalk from my pocket, desperately calculated the angle and flicked it as hard as I could towards ffawthawte's face. With an instanat reflex, she fired the Magnum and I flung myself aside, the upholstery of the chair exploding. Time seemed to stand still as the blue chalk sailed through the air and disappeared between ffawthawte's gaping lips, falling into her gullet with a satisfying plop.

On the television screen, a roar of applause greeted the conclusion of Lord Battenburg's address.

Meanwhile, Melissa ffawthawte was staggering on her pins and clutching at her throat. The Magnum clattered to the floor, and I was on my feet. Leaping across the couple of yards that separated us, I snatched Christmas, gripping the boy's wrist tightly.

'Daddy! Daddy!' cried the child.

'Don't you *Daddy* me, you vicious little shit!' I snarled, cracking him soundly across the buttocks. 'Now keep your mouth shut and do as you're told!'

He looked scared stiff, as well he might, and began to grizzle quietly.

Melissa ffawthawte's face was now as blue as the snooker chalk itself. She gestured helplessly towards me but I declined to assist.

'Sorry, dear,' I said. 'I'm all out of mercy.'

Gasping, squawking, she scrabbled at the door, threw it open and stumped out onto the gantry. I grabbed the chastened Christmas and raced after her.

Out in the dome, ffawthawte flapped her hands, trying desperately to attract attention. She gurgled and squeaked and clawed at her pretty throat but at last her green eyes dulled and rolled upward. With a horrible belch, she slid to the metal gantry floor, quite dead.

Christmas stared at her, mouth agape.

Far below, Lord Battenburg stepped back from the microphone, to allow the sickly form of Fetch Junior to take his place.

The bank of television screens had all lit up. Each showed different Scout huts – from Rangoon to Ramsgate, Tripoli to Timbuctoo – an excited crowd of children and parents, all poised with glasses in their hands.

Fetch's reedy tones rang out across the room: 'Scouts of all nations,' he cried. 'I invite you to raise your glasses and toast our beloved patron! I give you – Lord Battenburg!'

And suddenly I understood the missing link in this tangled skein. Images flashed through my brain. *A rainy churchyard. The delightful yet unobtainable Coral Beveridge. Liquorice sweets in fat, sweaty hands. And a rather tacky floral display, arranged to resemble a large bottle of fruit cordial, with a large letter M emblazoned on its front . . .*

'Christopher Miracle!' I ejaculated.

Now it made sense. The hostile takeover of his firm! A.C.R.O.N.I.M. needed the company because –

'Every single cup of orange squash,' I whispered in awe, 'in every single Scout hut . . . is laced with Black Butterfly!'

I shook my head in horror. A.C.R.O.N.I.M. didn't intend to kill Lord Battenburg. They were going to make him stand and watch as they poisoned half the world!

.19.
DIB-DIB-DEATH

'Stop it!' I yelled. 'Stop the broadcast!'

Heart pounding, I gripped the gantry banister. There was immediate consternation below and hundreds of faces turned up towards me. Playfair, recognising the old man in the black suit, groaned. 'Box!' he shouted. 'What the hell do you think you're doing?'

I threw a quick glance down at the blur of television screens. As far as I could see, the parents on view had all paused, glasses of squash in hand, and were gawping ahead, transfixed. 'This whole thing is a set-up!' I cried. 'The New Scout Movement – everything!'

Lord Battenburg swung round to confront my successor. 'What's going on?'

Playfair wiped the sweat from his brow and plastered a thin smile onto his face. 'The situation is entirely under control, sir—'

'Nonsense!' I hollered. 'You haven't the faintest idea. A.C.R.O.N.I.M. are—'

'Oh, not that again,' snarled Playfair. 'For God's sake!'

'It's true.' I rattled the steel banister in my desperation. Christmas stepped back, looking absolutely terrified. 'You have to believe me! The orange squash in all those Scout huts is laced with Black Butterfly. It will send millions of people off their heads, create worldwide panic . . .'

Playfair was speaking in urgent tones to the Scout bodyguard and gesticulating in my direction so I quickly turned my attention to Battenburg himself. 'The world is watching, your Lordship! You have it in your power to save them all. Tell them to throw away their drinks, I implore you!'

Lord Battenburg looked baffled. 'Orange squash?' he muttered.

'Yes!'

But, shaking his head, he turned back to the cameras. 'Please forgive this bizarre interruption, my friends. Now,' he looked down at Fetch Junior, who was simpering up at him, 'perhaps you would be so kind as to make the toast again?'

'It would be my pleasure,' hissed the miniature horror.

My heart sank.

And then, suddenly, one of the Scout bodyguard broke ranks. Although he looked pretty much identical to his fellows, in long shorts and wide-brimmed hat, there was no mistaking the sleek, athletic grace with which he bounded onto the platform.

Kingdom Kum!

With all around him frozen in shock, the boy neatly rugby-tackled Lord Battenburg, flattening him onto the dais. There was an instantaneous aria of screaming from the delegates and a high, petulant squealing from Fetch. 'No!' he rasped. 'No! No! No!'

The ugly little fellow hurled himself at Kingdom Kum, got him by the neck and the two of them rolled onto the floor. By now, the other Scouts had recovered from their moment of surprise, and, to a man, were rushing forward to help their leader. The direct attack on Lord Battenburg was something Allan Playfair had, of course, been waiting for. At a signal from him, his MI6 men sprang into action and raced towards Kingdom Kum. But the boy from the CIA managed to throw off Fetch Junior and, eyes glinting, he confronted the Service Chief.

'It's true, Playfair!' he rasped, rubbing at his reddened throat. 'Mr Box was right – you have to believe him!'

Fetch wriggled to his feet and glared at Kingdom, then snapped his fingers. Abandoning all pretence, the Scouts went for Playfair's men with a vengeance. Soon the chamber was a blur of fists and boots. Knives flashed and screams rang out as the two camps scrapped and tusseled over the polished floor.

Leaving Christmas behind, I stumbled hastily down the steel stairs from the gantry. The delegates began to surge towards the exit doors.

I threw a glance at the banks of television screens. Bewildered children and worried adults intently watched the carnage unfolding before them. But crucially, not one of them seemed to have raised their cup of orange squash to their lips!

I turned my attention back to the dais, where Kingdom Kum was locked in hand-to-hand fighting with an enormous Nordic-looking Scout. I ran over to help, only to spot Dr Fetch's misshapen offspring racing towards the cameras. Scrambling onto the dais, he stared down the lens, his chin jutting forward. 'Drink it!' he cried shrilly. 'Toast our Honorary Chairman! Drink it!'

But on every single screen, puzzled, frightened faces looked out at him. Suddenly, gunfire sprayed from the pitched battle that was raging nearby, and the screens exploded in a barrage of sparks and shattered glass. Playfair's men shot down three Scouts in one wave, their uniformed bodies jumping and twitching as bullets ripped through them.

'Fetch!' I called. 'Give it up!'

The mini-man snapped round towards me, eyes blazing with a loathing that was almost inhuman in its intensity. Then, with a shriek, he was on me.

He was appallingly strong. I gasped and gulped and wheezed as the nimble little fingers squeezed at my gullet. 'Now, old man, you're going to die!' he swore. 'Die for what you've done!'

I reached down and flailed at his body but it was hard and tightly muscled like a little armadillo. He managed a still-firmer grip around my throat. My head began to swim and I scrabbled desperately at the creature's shirt. At once my sweating fingers found his nipples, and I plunged my fingernails into them with all my strength.

Fetch screeched and wriggled in my grasp – but I knew I had

to hold on. Through dimming eyes, I could see blood beginning to stain the tawny fabric, forming little dartboards of gore. Again I pinched, feeling the soft skin give to the pressure of my nails.

At last, with a howl of pain, he let go of my neck and flopped to the floor, cupping his tiny palms over the damaged areas. I rubbed at my neck and staggered slightly, but knew I couldn't give the little monster an inch. All the villainous insanity of his father boiled within his veins.

Playfair staggered past, clutching a wounded arm, his face set and intense as he pumped his pistol into yet another Scout. For an instant, I was distracted, and then I gasped as Fetch Junior came at me again, this time brandishing a huge shard of broken glass from one of the smashed screens.

Lungs bursting, I turned and staggered back up the stairs I had only just descended.

My little son stood at the top, staring at me with his dark eyes. We were both now on the gantry, some thirty feet in the air.

'Go back!' I commanded. 'Go back into the room, Christmas. Get out of the way!'

He didn't move. I made to push him back into the viewing room but then his eyes widened and I swung round to see Fetch right behind me. He jabbed the lethal glass at me – once, twice. I ducked, but I was just too slow and the shard caught my thigh. Pain flashed through me. I yelled in agony.

'Years I've planned this! *Years!*' spat the hideous piglet.

'And you presume to undo all my work in a matter of minutes!'

'It's a knack,' I said breathlessly. 'Look, why . . . why don't you just drop it, you queer little thing? It's all . . . over.'

He nodded violently and sank his teeth into his lower lip. It was uncomfortably like looking at a barracuda. 'Oh yes, it's over, Box. For *you*.'

With that, Fetch shot like a torpedo towards me but I stuck out my wounded leg and he was flung headlong onto the gantry floor. The shard of glass leaped from his grip and clattered to rest just in front of Christmas's feet.

I shook my head to clear the spots from before my eyes.

Fetch Junior got to his feet, a little unsteadily. He threw a quick look at Christmas and thrust out his hot little hand. 'Give it to me, boy,' he demanded. 'The glass – throw it over here.'

Christmas's gaze flickered between me and his Akela, then he looked down at his shoes.

'*Do* it!' screamed Fetch. 'I order you!'

Christmas blinked and his lower lip began to tremble. The stunted Fetch positively vibrated with rage, but could come no nearer. Without Christmas to help him, he was unarmed.

I dashed forward to grab the glass and Fetch moved simultaneously. My shoe caught its jagged edge and it span across the gantry and sailed into empty air. I swung back towards him. Now we were more evenly matched!

Ignoring the swimming blackness in my mind and the searing pain in my wounded thigh, I clattered towards Fetch across the gantry and grabbed him under the armpits. At once he set to kicking me in the chest. The toe-caps of his tiny shoes hit home with horrible force, slamming into my ribs and catching me in the solar plexus. Then his hot little face rose before mine and his teeth were snapping at my cheek. I held on tight and stumbled to the edge of the walkway. Now his hands were scrabbling over my face, trying to locate my eyes. In moments, I knew, his thumbs would find their mark and plunge down into the sockets without mercy.

Faint with pain and the creature's weight, I swung Fetch over the banister so that he hung in mid-air. Now he was desperate to cling on, not wanting to risk me letting him go. So, like a terrified child, the hands that had been seeking to put out my eyes now scrambled to find purchase around my neck, and the nasty, thrashing legs wrapped themselves round my waist.

'Die, you little bastard!' I gasped, trying desperately to prise him off me.

Fetch shook his head wildly back and forth, sweat flicking from his soaked curls. 'No, no, *no*!' he spat. I pulled at his tiny frame, desperate to dislodge him, sagging with his weight as I tried to manoeuvre him into empty space. Still he clung on like some filthy squid. With my hands now free, I smashed him in the face with the heel of my palm.

'Get *off*!' I said, repeating the blow again and again. The rosebud mouth burst and blood gushed down his chin. And now the pale eyes filled up and he gazed at me in mute appeal.

'Please,' he whimpered, 'I don't want to die. Please, Mr Box. Please don't do this!'

It's not a child, I told myself, watching the split lip tremble and turn down in a clownish grimace. I shut my eyes and pushed him away from me with all my strength.

I felt his weight suddenly vanish.

Then I opened my eyes, expecting to see the little body tumbling down, down, down to the floor of the chamber. But there was no sign of him. I blinked. Then I gasped in surprise as I felt a tremendous tug at my ankles. I looked down to see Fetch hanging there, one reddening fist around my trouser leg, the other gripping the very edge of the gantry for grim death.

His eyes swivelled up and the look in them turned me cold. I read a dreadful, fatal determination there. Setting his jaw, he pulled with all his hideous strength and I felt myself topple towards the edge. If he were going, evidently I was too.

My stomach slammed into the gantry banister and I was instantly winded. My head swam and the room below telescoped up and down vertiginously.

Now Fetch was able to let go of my ankle and clasp his bloodied fingers into the wire mesh of the gantry. He was climbing back up!

'Enough!' I gasped and threw out my hand to grab his little head. Instead, my fingers groped and found something else. My spirits rose at once. His woggle!

Draped around his pallid neck lay the yellow neckerchief, now drenched in perspiration. Adrenalin and sheer bloody delight flooded through my aching body as I grasped the silky material in one hand and tightened the leather woggle with the other. With both hands grasping the mesh of the gantry, Fetch could do nothing. His pale eyes widened in horror as I pushed the knot tighter and tighter around his throat. He began to rattle and choke. Blood vessels erupted in his sickly yellow eyes like watercolour on blotting paper. Veins appeared on the flesh of the purpling face and a tracery of spittle foamed over the lips. Still I pushed on, a manic energy pulsing through me.

Then, suddenly, he went limp and his hands lost their grip on the gantry. I staggered for a second as I took the full burden of Akela's weight. Arms aching, I held him out over the yawning chasm, took one last look at the swollen, blackening face, its eyes turned upwards, tongue protruding grotesquely, and then let go.

The little uniformed body spiralled down. I watched it diminish until it thudded onto the metal floor far below, bounced comically and then came to rest.

I held onto the banister for I don't know how long, my head spinning, letting the breath seep slowly into my exhausted frame. At last, I felt a pressure on my hand and glanced wearily down to find Christmas staring up at me.

'Daddy,' he whimpered. 'I'm sorry. Will you . . . will you forgive me?'

I smiled at him and then slowly, very slowly, I let my face fall.

'No, I bloody well won't, you vindictive little bugger!' I cracked him across the backside and tears welled in his eyes. 'Don't think you're getting off that lightly. Now, get down those bloody stairs!'

By the time we stumbled down to the floor, it was all over. The few remaining Scouts stood huddled, leaderless and pathetic, rounded up by Playfair's squad.

The head of the newly combined MI6 and Royal Academy looked rather ill, blinking at the utter chaos that surrounded him. 'B-Box, old love,' he stammered. 'I'm so . . . I mean, what can I say?'

I nodded companionably to him. 'Dear me, Allan. What a mess.' I glanced down at my watch. 'Oh, for shame. I'm retired. Looks like it's all yours.'

Limping towards Kingdom Kum, who was supervising the restraint of the errant Scouts.

'Hey,' he said gently. 'You okay?'

I nodded. 'You believed me?'

'Sure, baby!' he grinned. '*Eventually*. I knew there was something weird about those blond goons in the hospital. Besides, like I told you before, I respect tradition. You were the best. You still are.'

I managed an exhausted chuckle.

'Then,' continued Kingdom, 'all I had to do was use my famous charms and boyish looks to infiltrate these characters, and – hey, what is it?'

I had winced as the pain in my leg flared again. Kingdom dropped to his knees and his long, slim hands were soon all over my thigh. He caught Christmas's eye and winked. 'Who's this little guy?'

'The fruit of my loins,' I muttered. 'Comprehensively withered on the vine.'

Kingdom laughed. 'You don't say!' He looked the child up

and down. 'Gonna be a heartbreaker,' he cooed. 'Like his Poppa.'

I held out my hands and pulled Kingdom to his feet. We looked at each other. 'I'm going to need a little rest and recuperation,' I said at last. 'Care to join me?'

Kingdom giggled his sing-song giggle. 'Sure, baby. If you promise *not* to behave.'

I held up my hand. 'Scout's honour.'

.20.
THE LAST LUCIFER

The afternoon sky outside the window was fresh as paint, a wonderful hazy blue streaked with jet trails. I was in a certain Palace at the end of a certain Mall, the flapping flag on its pole indicating that a certain personage was *in*.

The young queen stood before me, arse exposed.

'Blimey!' he cried. 'You're a caution!'

'Well, to coin a phrase,' I said, running my hand through the footman's Brylcreemed locks, 'you've never had it so good.'

The young man (his name was Dennis, I think. Or Desmond) and I were in the throne room. Not *the* throne room, of course. This one, despite its dado railing and creamy Georgian hue, was disappointingly functional. I ran my fingers over the curve of his buttocks and kissed him, far more interested in his surly charms than the prospect of that afternoon's pomp.

There was an urgent knocking at the lavatory door.

'Mr Box? Mr Box, sir, are you quite all right?'

I pulled Dennis or Desmond closer. 'Just . . . coming!' I said brightly.

The mortified young man turned quite scarlet and pulled up his tight trousers. 'Don't give us away,' he warned me. 'I'll get the push.'

The elderly flunky outside the cubicle cleared his throat and said ponderously, 'Her Majesty is waiting, sir.'

I kissed the boy, and then helped him to clamber onto the toilet seat. 'Number Nine, Downing Street,' I whispered in his neat little ear. 'Pop over later. I'll be . . . entertaining.'

He grinned happily. 'So will I. *Promise*.'

I opened the cubicle door and shut it carefully behind me to obscure the footman's crouched form. I moved to the wash-basin and caught sight of my reflection. Not in bad nick, I concluded, given the bashing I'd recently received. And there was a glint back in those cold blue eyes that I rather liked.

I followed the other, less appealing servant out into the damask-lined corridor. Champagne glasses tinkled, medals shone and the susurration of small talk was like the roar of the Jamaican surf.

And then, though my shiny shoes sank deep into the thick pile of the carpet, my thoughts were drifting far, far away. I was back in a hammock, strung between two curved palms on a white beach, the blue flash of a parrot fluttering into the branches above, a lizard scuttling by, quicksilver fast. Kingdom Kum lay facing me, opening one eye and leaning over the side of the hammock to grab a freshly opened bottle of Mouton-Rothschild. My fingers were running over the arch of his brown back and I felt the tender touch of the boy's kisses on my neck. Then his warm body locking against mine, wonderful, comfortable . . .

I was pulled back to reality as I spotted, squeezed comically into a morning suit, the immense form of Whitley Bey. He had a spindly glass swamped in one great paw and was deep in conversation with a servant. I moved closer.

'What – *none*?' he was saying.

'No, sir.'

'No beer *at all*?'

'Not even for ready money,' I said, steering him away by the elbow. 'They don't run to Newcastle Brown at Buckingham Palace, Whitley.'

'I'm not asking for that, man,' he opined. 'Just something other than this cat's widdle. Anyway . . .' He looked me up and down, grinning. 'How the hell are ya?'

'I'm fine,' I said at last. 'Just dandy. Enjoying my retirement.'

'Haddaway and shite, man,' muttered Whitley. 'You'll never retire.'

'No, no,' I said. 'It's true. I'm perfectly sanguine about it. Everything's been handed over to Allan Playfair and the Service. I've hung up my pistol for good.'

'That no-mark get,' sniffed the big man. 'Bloody hell, if the Secret Service is in the hands of buggers like him, God help us.'

'Oh, he'll be all right,' I said charitably. 'I think he learned a lesson or two with the Black Butterfly business. And he's handled the mopping up rather well.'

'Oh, aye?'

'Yes. The New Scout Movement has been thoroughly

purged. Comprehensive re-education for all the poor little sods they indoctrinated.'

Whitley Bey sipped gingerly at his champagne. He pulled a face. 'Including your young 'un?'

'Most definitely. Then it's off to his new school. It is to be hoped that the austere regime there might instil something worthwhile into the little brute.'

'What if it doesn't?'

'Oh, he'll probably end up joining the Army and taking out his fascist tendencies on the natives of some obscure British Dependency. Doesn't matter, so long as he finds his own way. That's what I did. And, in any case, I shan't be around to see it.'

'What do you mean?'

'I mean, I'm not getting any younger, Whitley.'

'Bollocks, man,' he guffawed. 'You're bloody indestructible, you.'

'You're too kind.' I steered a waiter in my direction and liberated a bottle of Mumm.

'What are you gonna do with yourself?' asked Whitley.

I shrugged. 'Paint pictures. That was always my first love.' I caught a glimpse of Dennis or Desmond, slipping into the room as unobtrusively as he could manage, adjusting his waistcoat. 'Well,' I admitted. 'Maybe my *second* love.'

Whitley followed my gaze. The sovereign screwed into his eye socket caught the light from one of the room's great chandeliers and twinkled. 'Anyone in mind? To sit for you, like, I mean?' He nudged me, painfully, in the ribs. 'That lad, eh – Kingdom whatsit. You got pretty close, by all accounts.'

'Gone back to the States,' I murmured. 'Duty called.'

'I see,' said Whitley. 'That's a shame.'

I nodded. Yes, it was. But I'd get over it. I always did. 'Probably for the best. Given my newly exalted status.'

'Hell, aye! *Sir* Lucifer Box,' he grinned. 'What do you think of that?'

'Insultingly tardy,' I said. 'But better late than never.'

'You been here before? The Palace?'

'Well, naturally,' I said. 'When you've been around as long as I have. Though, I once missed out on a hand-shandy from Prince Eddie because I couldn't choose between a gardenia and a carnation for my buttonhole.'

'I never know when you're being serious or not.'

'You can safely assume, usually *not*.'

Suddenly Whitley Bey grabbed the champagne bottle from me, and shook his great head. 'No more of that, petal. I think it's time.'

'Time?'

He nodded towards the throne-room doors which had just opened. Ahead, at the end of a long, red carpet, sat young Bess.

The Second, that is.

The elderly flunky appeared at my elbow and raised his eyebrows. I drained the last of my Mumm. 'Well,' I said. 'Here goes.'

Then I was processing slowly down the carpet towards the throne. I didn't look at the Queen as I knelt, but winced a little at the kindling-crackle of my joints. I felt the light touch of the sword and then I got to my feet.

It was only then that I realised quite how lovely the young girl was. Those eyes! That pursed but foxy mouth. That glossy dark hair . . .

'Sir Lucifer,' she said quietly. 'One has heard such a lot about you.'

'Really, Ma'am? From whom?'

Her Majesty gestured towards another regal personage, seated on her left. I started.

It was her mother, and suddenly, in the soft radiance of that opulent room, I saw the familiar features in an altogether different light. The years fell away.

Armistice Night! 1918! Fox-trotting across the floor at Maxim's and – well, now, I remembered. Pink champagne, a fumbled brassiere, the well-cushioned embrace of the future Duchess . . .

I met her twinkling gaze and bless me if the old girl didn't wink.

I smiled what my friends call, naturally enough, the smile of Lucifer.